endgame

endgame

Nancy Garden

Harcourt, Inc.

ORLANDO   AUSTIN   NEW YORK   SAN DIEGO   TORONTO   LONDON

www.HarcourtBooks.com

Library of Congress Cataloging-in-Publication Data
Garden, Nancy.
Endgame/Nancy Garden.—1st ed.
p. cm.
Summary: Fourteen-year-old Gray Wilton, bullied at school and
ridiculed by an unfeeling father for preferring drums to hunting,
goes on a shooting rampage at his high school.
[1. Bullies—Fiction. 2. High schools—Fiction. 3. Schools—Fiction.
4. Family problems—Fiction.] I. Title.
PZ7.G165End 2006
[Fic]—dc22 2005019486
ISBN-13: 978-0-15-205416-8 ISBN-10: 0-15-205416-2

Text set in Bembo
Designed by Cathy Riggs

First edition
A C E G H F D B

Printed in the United States of America

3448 4781

10/06

For **D. P.**, who didn't

With heartfelt thanks to Jan McClain, an English teacher from Chatfield Senior High School in Littleton, Colorado, who believed this book needed to be written and who encouraged me to write it.

My thanks also to the editors whose comments helped me find the way to tell this story and, most of all, to my enormously supportive and perceptive Harcourt editor, Karen Grove.

Thanks, too, to Chris Jovanelli Jr., for answering my questions about drums. Any errors that remain are mine, not his!

endgame

Prologue

Juvenile Detention Center

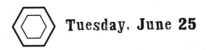 **Tuesday, June 25**

Hexagons.

Six sides.

The wire mesh embedded in the window glass formed little six-sided figures.

Yeah, hexagons.

Gray stared at them.

But so what? It didn't matter.

Nothing much mattered anymore. Had it ever?

Yeah, maybe. Long ago.

The glass was so thick and dirty that by a trick of light, Gray could see his reflection in it, in hexagon after hexagon.

It made him mad that the secure rooms, the ones like his, had wire hexagons in the window glass and dead bolts in the heavy steel doors, and that the doors had little steel sliding windows so they could spy on you and shove food through without coming in, like you were too dirty to get close to. It made him even madder that the secure rooms were right on the quad. That was extra torture, probably on purpose, so when you heard the other losers playing basketball you had to remember that you weren't going to get outside till they finally scheduled your trial.

Losers.

Six sides to a hexagon.

How many sides to a loser?

How many sides to me?

Son, brother. Friend? Archer. Drummer.

That's five.

What about six? The sixth side.

Come on, the sixth side!

As if he were dreaming, Gray saw his reflected face morph into Lindsay's: friendly, then worried, then scared; then into Zorro's: disdainful, jeering, finally incredulous.

Son, brother, friend? Archer. Drummer.

Murderer.

Wednesday, June 26

The steel door clanked, wrenching Gray from sleep. He groaned and sat up on the plank that served as a bed, rubbing his eyes.

A guard stood in the doorway. "Upsy daisy, kiddo," he said, reaching for Gray's arm. "You got a visitor. Better wake up; it's your lawyer."

Gray shook his head, then shoved lank blond hair out of his eyes. *Shit,* he thought as the guard propelled him into the corridor and along it to a small square room bare of everything except a table and two chairs. On one of the chairs sat a stout, pleasant-faced, balding man. *Shit!*

The man stood up and held out his hand. Gray stared at the black hairs sprouting between each pair of knuckles. *Werewolf,* he thought with a sardonic smile, remembering a movie he'd once seen. He didn't take the offered hand.

The man moved back to his chair and gestured Gray to the other one. "Have a seat," he said. "I'm Sam Falco. I think they told you that your dad hired me to represent you?"

Gray, still standing, nodded. He felt sleepy again.

"Have a seat," Mr. Falco said again, and Gray, reluctantly—what else was there to do?—did.

Mr. Falco rubbed his hairy hands together. Then he pulled a long yellow lined pad and two sharp yellow pencils out of the briefcase that Gray now saw was beside his chair. "I need to know what happened, son," he said gently. "I need to know how you see it. And I need to know what led up to it. You'd moved, hadn't you, nine or ten months before the, er, event, right?"

Gray nodded silently.

"You're going to have to talk to me, Gray," Mr. Falco said. "We want to make sure you're treated fairly. I can't argue for that in court unless I know about you and about everything that happened. I've got a terrible memory, so I'm going to record what we both say. That way I won't forget anything."

Mr. Falco bent down and pulled a fancy-looking cassette tape recorder out of his briefcase. "Don't mind this," he said, popping in a cassette. "Ignore it and just talk. No, wait. Wait'll I turn it on . . ."

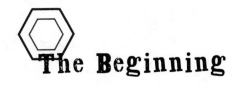

The Beginning

FALCO: Sam Falco interviewing Grayson Wilton, age fifteen, at South Juvenile Detention Center, case number 9872. Gray, I've told you about the tape recorder. Am I right that you have no objections to it? . . . Gray?

GRAY: Yeah, okay. I guess. I don't really care.

FALCO: Okay. Thank you. So—I guess we might as well get started. Let's see—okay, when did you move to Connecticut?

GRAY: Last summer. August? Around the middle.

FALCO: Go on.

GRAY: What? Go on where? With what?

FALCO: Well—how about your new place? What's the first thing you remember doing there? Unpacking? Exploring?

GRAY: No. Mowing. I remember cutting the grass. Yeah, and counting . . .

One hundred and fifty-three steps, big ones, from the house to the street, and one hundred and seventy-five from side to side. That was our front lawn in Green-ford, Connecticut, which my mother made me mow almost as soon as we moved into our new house. I guess that makes it twenty-six thousand, seven hun-dred and seventy-five square steps big.

Mowing's not too bad of a job, so I didn't mind much, even though I was in a sort of bad mood about moving. Hopeful, too, though.

I stopped counting and made up one of those whatchamacallits, you know, mantras? *Gonna be bet-ter, gonna be better* here; *gonna be better, gonna be better* here. That got pretty lame, though, so I stopped and tried to blank my mind, but now it kept wanting to go *mow, mow, mow your*—what? I couldn't think of what. Not boat. Grass? Yard?

By the time I'd run out of mind games and was pretty sweaty, this girl came over from next door carrying a dish, like a one-girl Welcome Wagon. She was like, "Hi, I'm Lindsay Maller, from next door. My mom made a casserole for you guys. You know, welcome to the neighborhood, welcome to Green-ford, Connecticut, too."

I knew she was trying to make conversation, but I was worried she'd be able to smell me from ten feet—no, wrong, back to counting: ten *steps*—away, so I just told her my mom was inside and went back to counting and mowing. By the time I was done I was really thirsty, so I went in to get a drink and I saw the girl was sitting at the kitchen table with my brother, Peter. Mom was handing out Cokes and I wanted to get one, too, but I was still sweaty and the girl was right there. I was trying to decide whether to go in anyway or get some water from the bathroom when I heard Mom say, "So, you must be—what? Sixteen?"

"Yes, sixteen," the girl said.

"Peter's seventeen and Grayson—Gray, my other son—is fourteen. I don't suppose you have a little brother?"

"No, sorry," she said. "A sister, Joni. She's eight."

"Too young for Gray," Mom said, "even though he's small and young for his age." She dropped her voice almost like she knew I was there. "You know—immature."

Well, how could I go in then? I could feel my face getting red and my sort-of bad mood getting really bad. I forgot about being thirsty, and I really wanted to bang on my drums, which is what sometimes helped when I was mad. But my drums weren't set up yet and I couldn't get at them anyway, so I ran back outside, shoved the lawn mower into the garage, and rummaged in the U-Haul for my target and bow and arrows, thinking, *Damn, why'd she say that about me being small and immature? Can't my own mother tell I'm not done growing?* Jemmy—he was my best friend back in Massachusetts—grew a lot that year all of a sudden, and when we moved, his mom was still kidding about how she had to keep buying him new jeans.

Then I said to myself, *Chill, Gray. Gonna be better, gonna be better* here, *remember? Hey, maybe my zits might even go away this year.*

Yeah, in my dreams.

Dad never did really come right out and tell the truth about why we had to move to Connecticut. What he *said* was it'd be an easy commute into New York City to his new job. But he didn't have to get a new job. There wasn't anything wrong with his old one. He's some kind of supervisor at a business-machine company. That's what he did at his old job, too, so what's the big difference? "More money, guys" was what he told us, though, and he gave my brother, Peter, one of his chip-off-the-old-block punches. "More money for college for my Number-One Son."

Maybe you noticed that he didn't say anything about his Number-Two Son. See, I was the real reason for the new job and the move, and the reason both Mom and Dad seemed to be waiting for me to screw up again, and the reason why we never had any fun as a family, all four of us, anymore.

We used to do stuff on weekends, like a normal family. The zoo, hikes, museums. We even went to Disney World when I was little. That was fun. Neat rides and stuff. And we once all stood outside the fence at this little racetrack and watched ten races from there because kids weren't allowed inside where there was betting going on. But we bet each other, and I won a dollar.

No more, though.

But things'll be better here, I told myself. *I'm gonna change. We all are. Mom's gonna stand up to Dad more, and Dad's gonna stop getting on my case, and Perfect Peter's gonna make a mistake once in a while, and I'm gonna stop making mistakes. Change for the better, you know?*

Yeah.

I tried to feel it in my—bones, I guess. Isn't that where people are supposed to feel things like that?

Like that's really possible!

I'd found my archery stuff by then, and my dog, Barker—he was a brown and white springer spaniel—was looking at me from where he was sitting in the driveway. He stretched his front legs out and sent his rump up like dogs do when they want to play.

"Come watch me shoot," I told him. I lugged the target to the backyard and set it up. "Let's go get us some bull's-eyes."

I did get some, too, and Barker watched, grinning like he always did. He'd tried to chase my arrows a couple of times back when he was a puppy, but as soon as he saw that they pretty much always went into the target, he stopped. And this time was no different. By the time Dad drove in, back from whatever had sent him to the hardware store, there was a whole cluster of arrows sticking out of the center of the target. I felt better, too.

"You oughta move that target back some, Gray," Dad called almost before he was all the way out of the car. "Make it harder for yourself."

That was it. Nothing about the bull's-eyes. No "Nice shooting" or "Way to go, kid," like he used to say. As soon as he'd told me to move the target, Dad lumbered into the house, carrying a paper bag of whatever he'd dashed out for.

Okay, so then my mantra about things getting better did a nosedive out of my head and I slammed my hand against the target, nearly knocking it over and making Barker look up from the sun patch he was snoozing in. As I started to yank the arrows out I heard Peter yell, "Hey, don't wreck it!"

My big brother—people say he looks like Dad and I look like Mom—came out the back door, gave Barker a pat on the head as he passed, and then slapped me on the back. He's like, "Wow," as he examined what was left of the arrow cluster. "Have to start calling you Robin Hood." He pulled out the rest of the arrows and handed them to me. "How about a run? Mom says we're going out for dinner. We've got time to explore. Although," he said, sort of wagging his head at the street, "it looks to me as if there's not a whole lot to see." He slapped me on the back again. "C'mon anyway. Let's go change."

◇ ◇ ◇

I was still mad when we started, but I calmed down some after Peter and Barker and I had been running along the boring suburban streets for a while. I had to admit Pete sure was right about there not being much to see. But, hey, it wasn't as if I really cared about the neighborhood, not much, anyway. Back home where we'd lived in Massachusetts, the houses were older, bigger, more settled-looking—more like city houses. Okay, people's yards were small, not many square steps to them, but they looked as if they'd been there for a hundred years, plenty of time to grow patches of grass and thick bushes. Some of the fancier houses had porches and bay windows and were snuggled, kind of, into their yards, with cushiony shrubbery around them. And our house was on a corner with lots of bushes and trees between us and the other houses, so Dad let me practice my drums as long as I stuck to the schedule he'd worked out with the neighbors. I think the trees and bushes muffled the sound a little; at least no one ever complained.

But here, the trees were spindly and the bushes were little and thin. Most of the houses were the same. They either had the front door to the left of a big window or the front door to the right of it, and they all had front paths with a slight curve to the right or left depending on which side of the big window the door was on. The streets all had the same kind of slight curve as the house paths did and they sort of melted into each other when they met.

"Whew!" Peter turned his head toward me as we ran past a house with its door on the left. "Remind me not to live in a place like this when I grow up."

I laughed. "When I grow up" had been a family joke ever since I was, like, six or seven. I'd gotten so mad when some relative asked me for the hundredth time what I wanted to do when I grew up that I'd said, "Only little kids talk about that," and everyone laughed like crazy, since, you know, I *was* a little kid. It was kind of nice hearing an old family joke when we'd just moved to a new place. A good sign, maybe. Can an old family joke revive an old family? In the past, though, that joke had kind of pissed me off. It had reminded me that Peter knew what he wanted to do and I wasn't sure, and that reminded me of Dad's saying lately that I should start thinking about "practical careers." That's what he called the kinds of things he thought were the "right" jobs. Peter was going to be a doctor and find the cure for cancer that would have saved Grandma's life if she'd waited for him to get through his education before she'd gotten sick. Dad thought that was great—"My son the doctor," you know? One of the "right jobs." But I knew that what I probably wanted to do was sure as heck not a "right job," and Dad wouldn't want to acknowledge it, let alone brag about it, even if I got really good at it, like famous. "My son the drummer? My son the songwriter?"

Yeah, right!

I knew I wanted to do something really big, anyway. Maybe drumming and songwriting wouldn't be it, but that was the closest I'd gotten.

"Yeah," I said to Peter. "Remind me not to live in a place like this, too."

By then we'd run to the end of our street, which swept around to the right, and then we'd turned right twice more, making a sort of curvy square.

"I'll be damned," Peter said, stopping and nearly bumping into Barker, who'd chosen that moment to take a detour in front of us. "We should be back, but we're not."

"Maybe we're lost," I said. "Maybe we'll never get back. Maybe we're in a time warp."

Peter gave me a look. "Smart-ass," he said. "Anyone ever tell you how weird you are?"

"You're weirder." I squatted and flopped one of Barker's ears over. "Home, James," I said into it.

Barker wagged his tail and sat down.

"Big help he is," Peter said. "I guess we'd better go back the way we came."

I nodded and we U-turned, retracing our steps and ending up in front of the house next door just as that girl, whose name I thought I remembered was Linda, or something like that, came out.

"Well, hi there," Peter said in the fake surprised way he reserved for girls he wanted to get to know. "Hi, again, Lindsay!"

Lindsay, that's it, I thought. I faded into the scenery, partly because of not wanting her to remember what Mom had said about me, partly because of not wanting her to smell me, and partly because when Peter started talking to a girl, the only thing one could do anyway was wait it out. Girls always noticed him; he was kind of a hunk, with lots of thick brown hair and Dad's "strong jaw" and what people call a "cleft chin." Once I heard some girl say he was "drop-dead gorgeous."

The less said about how I looked back then—and

I guess still do—the better. Skinny. Okay, small, like Mom said to Linda-Lindsay. Limp, dirty blond hair. Nerdy, I guess. Hey, at least I don't wear glasses!

"Hi, again, Peter. And Gray," the Lindsay-girl was saying.

I said, "Hi." I had to admit she had a cute smile, and she had kind of a cute nose, too. No zits, either.

Okay, I guess I didn't mention that I had about a million of them. Still do, some anyway, but back then, every place there wasn't a zit, seems like there was a scab from me trying to pop one, or a scar from one I'd already popped.

No one said anything for a minute. I wondered if I should, but I couldn't think of what.

"Do you run a lot?" Lindsay finally asked, looking at Peter, of course.

"Nah," Peter told her, like running didn't matter to him, which I guess was true, but he did it a lot anyway. "Just now and then, when I feel like it. It's basketball and baseball I really go for. Mostly I run to keep in shape and, I don't know, just to run."

"Basketball and baseball?" Lindsay said. "Maybe I'll see you play. I go to the games sometimes. And there's a good music teacher, Gray," she added as I moved away with Barker. "Peter told me you write songs."

"Yeah," I said, although I was kind of mad at Peter for talking about me. I mean, what else had he told her there in our new kitchen? But I said, "I play drums, too," and then I decided to make a joke of it. "That's my sport. Well, that and archery. But drumming's a real workout. You know, for the hands. Feet, too, actually." I kind of mimicked drumming for a second, even tapping my foot like I was hitting a bass, but I could tell right away that the joke wasn't funny. I guess the way it came out, it wasn't even really a joke.

But Lindsay laughed anyway, like she was being polite. "You looked pretty good running," she said. "You both did." She turned back to Peter, stooped, and gave Barker a pat. "Him, too."

I saw the front door to our new house-like-all-the-other-houses open, and Dad stuck his head out. "Boys!" he called. "Your mother says you've got just enough time to shower before we go out to dinner."

FALCO: What happened to the casserole that girl brought over? How was it?

GRAY: I think we had it the next night. It was okay, I guess. I really don't remember.

FALCO: Can you tell me about dinner that first night? Must've been kind of a celebration, in a new place and all. Or was it? Do you remember it?

GRAY: Yeah, maybe sort of a celebration . . .

We went to this fancy place. Dad wanted me and Pete to wear ties and jackets 'cause he and Mom were getting dressed up. We grubbed around for them, me and Pete, but we sort of accidentally-on-purpose couldn't find them. Even Perfect Peter went along with that. So we got away with good sport shirts instead.

Mom and Dad had some kind of drinks, and Dad let Peter have a sip of his when the waiter wasn't looking. Not me, though. I didn't want it anyway. Well, not much. I'd tasted booze once and I really didn't like it.

Dad made a toast about new beginnings, a new job for him and one for Mom—Mom's a nurse—a new school for me and Pete, and what he called new opportunities for us all. Then he looked kind of significantly at me and said, "Right, Grayson?" and I said, "Right, Dad." It felt like sort of a vow, like King Arthur and a knight from this book I had when I was a little kid, about—what was it?—the Round Table. I really meant it, too, what I said. I really hoped I could do it.

Mom and Dad had fancy hors d'oeuvres, some fishy thing in shells, and Pete and I had some cheesy thing—no, not *cheesy*—I mean made out of cheese. And we all had steaks, and Mom and Dad had wine.

Dad gave Pete a little of that, too. As usual, I was too young. "Next year," he said.

Yeah.

But it was kind of fun and kind of happy and hopeful, mostly, except at the end when we got home and I was going to bed. Dad came into my room then and said, "New beginnings, Gray. Here's your chance. A new start in a new place. Remember that."

As if I hadn't already thought about it a lot!

I told him yeah, I'd make a new start, but it was kind of weird, like what if I slipped up and the slipup wasn't my fault or was just a dumb mistake? There didn't seem to be much room for any mistakes at all, and it was kind of like he didn't think I was going to do the right thing anyway.

I wanted to, though. I really did.

FALCO: Good, Gray. What next? Go on.

Yeah, well, not much happened till school started. We went to church Sunday—Good Shepherd, I think it was called. It was pretty boring. Mom was all excited about this youth group Peter wanted to go to. Guess who was in it? Right. Lindsay-from-next-door. Mom said she wanted me to go, too, but luck-ily it wasn't going to start for a while. I mean, I've got nothing against church or religion or anything, but to me it's a private thing. And even back then I had a lot of trouble working out stuff like how God could really pay attention to what every person in the whole world was thinking and doing and praying for. He hadn't ever seemed to pay a lot of attention to me when I'd prayed, and he'd never seemed to help me much. He sure didn't later, either, come to think of it.

There was a whole week till school started, and Mom spent a lot of time unpacking and arranging stuff in the new house—she seemed pretty happy doing that—and Dad went to his new job, and Peter helped Mom some and talked to that new girl from next door, and he ran a lot. Me? I helped Mom, too, maybe more than Pete did, hanging curtains and moving boxes around and stuff, and I took Barker for lots of walks and fooled around with my guitar and set up my drums and shot a lot of arrows and took Barker for more walks and tried not to notice when Dad started talking about going hunting.

See, Dad got Barker to be a hunting dog, but the Christmas he gave him to me and Peter (even though it was pretty obvious Dad wanted him to be *his* dog), Barker, who was just a tiny puppy, came bounding right over to me and lapped his tongue all over my face and made me laugh more than I guess I'd ever laughed before or have since. Okay, Dad was the one who gun-trained him, but I was the one who took him to puppy school and taught him the basic stuff, like sit and stay and come, and heel and down. He was good at it, too. And most of the time, I was the one who fed him, so he was pretty much my dog, and kind of my best friend, besides my friend Jemmy in Massachusetts who I'd known since we were little kids.

It made me mad that Barker kind of liked hunting, at least he seemed to.

Anyway, it was mostly a pretty boring week. I began to feel kind of bad again about being in Greenford, Connecticut, and I missed my friend Jemmy, so I called him a couple times. He told me he'd been doing all the stuff we used to do, only with some other kids, and that made me feel worse. Barker was great when I was feeling like that.

FALCO: Feeling like what?

GRAY: Huh?

FALCO: Barker was great when you were feeling how?

GRAY: Sad. You know. Like, like kind of down.
    Lonely, maybe, wanting to talk to someone,
    only there wasn't anyone there, or it wasn't
    something I could talk about to anyone, not
    even to Jemmy.

FALCO: What would Barker do?

GRAY: He'd be there, you know what I mean? When
no one else was. He'd jump on my bed and lick
my face, and then if I didn't laugh, he'd just
snuggle up next to me and let me hang on to
him. He even let me wipe my eyes with his ears.

FALCO: When you were crying?

GRAY: Well . . . maybe. Maybe a little, like once or
twice.

FALCO: It's okay, Gray. Guys cry . . . Okay, tell me
about the rest of that boring week.

GRAY: Yeah, okay . . .

Mom took me to buy school clothes toward the end
of the week. She let Pete buy his by himself, but me
she had to take. I don't care a whole lot about clothes,
but there ought to be a school to teach mothers how
to buy clothes for their kids, at least when their kids
are boys. She was mostly okay about jeans, but she
wanted me to wear these really dorky prep-type polo
shirts, and we had a big fight about that, so we ended
up not buying anything, and I wore my favorite blue
Third Wheel T-shirt to school the first day. In case
you don't know, Third Wheel is this really cool band
with the best drummer in the world in it. I think so,
anyway.

Oh, yeah, that was the other thing. Like I said, I'd
fooled around with my guitar, but I'd also unpacked

my drums and set them up in this sort of blocked-off room in the cellar, where Dad said I could practice, but he said I couldn't till he'd checked it out with the neighbors. I was kind of pissed when he said that, especially since he didn't seem in any hurry to talk to them about it. It had already been too long since I'd been able to practice. I finally got him to let me work with practice pads—in case you don't know, they mute the sound—but that's so not the same.

FALCO: How often did you usually practice? You know, before you moved?

GRAY: A lot, man! Every day. See, in Massachusetts we had this neat garage with a sort of loft, I guess you'd call it. And I had my drums up there. It was kind of hard getting them up and down when I took them to school the few times I did, but Jemmy's dad had this truck, and he used to drive us to practice, so he'd take them when I had to get them there. Jemmy played clarinet. I played the school drums most of the time. They were okay. Not as good as mine, but okay.

FALCO: I had flute lessons when I was in school. But I hated practicing.

GRAY: Wow, I can't imagine that! Practicing's great! And drums are so cool, the best. They, I don't know, they make me really . . . alive, I guess,

sort of. That's weird, I know. But nothing
bothers me when I'm practicing.

FALCO: I bet you're a pretty good drummer, too.

GRAY: Yeah, maybe. I guess.

FALCO: I'd like to hear more about your music
sometime. But I guess we'd better talk about
school. How was the first day? How'd you get
there, by the way? Did your dad drive you? Or
did you walk, take the bus, what?

GRAY: Bus . . .

When I looked out the window, I saw this bus
pulling away from the curb. I was afraid I might be
about to start my new school career by being late, so
even though I was half asleep, I ran out the door. But
by then the bus was gone, and I saw Peter standing
there with Lindsay; it turned out that bus wasn't the
high school one.

I wondered what high school was going to be
like. Better than middle school, I told myself. Maybe
lots better.

Yeah. That's what I was planning anyway.

As soon as I was out the door, Lindsay yelled,
"Gray! Over here." She pulled a piece of paper out
of her pocket and was showing it to Peter when I got
up to them. "Hi, Gray," she said.

She looked really nice, with her hair shiny clean

and a sort of long greenish sweater that fit really closely around her body.

"Nervous?" she asked. "I sure was on my first day of high school."

I *was* nervous, but how could I say that? So I just sort of shrugged.

"Well, I'm nervous," Peter said. "Or I was till I met my personal guide." He made a little bow at Lindsay.

Lindsay laughed and started to bow back, I guess, but her pack tried to slip off and Peter caught it and bowed again.

That was such an, I don't know, intimate little scene with no room for me in it that I moved away, and then a big yellow bus came around the corner so I yelled, "Is that the bus?"

"No, it's the middle school one," Lindsay called back. "Hey, Gray?"

I turned around.

"My best friend Hannah's sister is a freshman, too. Kathy Roget. She's nice."

"Yeah, cool," I said. I could feel my face getting red, like she was trying to hook me up with her or something, so I walked away, trying to be invisible, and sat down on the curb till the bus came. When it did, I got on fast, still being invisible.

I thought maybe invisibility would be helpful till

I had a chance to figure out how things worked at Greenford High.

I walked to the back of the bus and slid quickly into the first empty seat next to a window, ignoring a few stares. *Maybe I'll be a chemist,* I thought, *and invent an invisibility potion.*

Sure. With my average, be a chemist.

No, wait, I thought. *I forgot. I'm gonna work on that. Do homework on time, get my marks up. Stay cool.*

Very much stay cool. Very cool.

I looked out the window. More identical houses. Left door, right door, left door, right door—whoa! We'd just passed a subversive one with the door in the middle and windows on both sides.

I tried to remember a song Mom used to sing about houses looking like ticky-tacky little boxes. Whatever it was, it sure seemed to fit Greenford, Connecticut.

But it's not about the neighborhood, I told myself. Okay, so it *is* about going to high school for the first time and doing that in a new town. Whenever I tried to imagine that, though, my throat sort of closed up and my hands and my armpits got sweaty and I had to go back to my "gonna be better" mantra.

When a green car went by, I noticed it was a Ford, so I concentrated on wondering how many green Fords there were in Greenford, Connecticut.

There should have been lots, but I didn't see any more.

The bus made a bunch of stops. Then, when it was almost filled up, it went through a fancy neighborhood where the houses actually almost had personalities, and this kid in a camouflage jacket, black pants, and a turned-around khaki baseball cap got on and eased into the still-empty seat next to me like he owned it. Longish hair as black as his pants was spewing out from under his cap.

"You're new," he said.

"Yeah. Last I looked." I turned back to the window.

The boy nodded. "Cool. Someone from The Outside."

I turned again. "The Outside?"

"Yeah, you know. Not one of the inmates." The boy held up his hand. "Ross Terrel."

I wasn't sure what he wanted me to do with his hand, if anything, so I told him my name instead.

Ross used his hand to scratch his head like that was what he meant all along. "You a freshman? New in town?"

I nodded.

"You like computers?"

I shrugged. "Don't know."

Ross stared like I'd grown vampire teeth. "You mean you don't have one?"

Here we go again, I thought. I hated explaining this. "My dad does. He doesn't let me use it. Just my brother." I didn't add that Dad blacklisted me after I'd mistakenly deleted his financial files last March, which, as I guess you know, isn't long before tax time.

Ross didn't pursue that, which made me think he might be okay. "That's tough," he said. "Tell you what. At the high school, I bet there'll be computers in the library. We could look, anyway. Lunchtime, maybe. Or later, after school."

This sounded promising, but I didn't want to seem too eager. One thing I learned in my last school was that you can't be too careful.

Still . . .

"What about the bus?" I asked. "Won't it have left?"

"There's lots of buses from the high school, man. Lots of buses."

So on we went, out of the fancy neighborhood and up a hill, and finally the bus turned into this parking lot next to a low, mostly brick building. I could see a sidewalk leading from the parking lot to one of those half-moon-type driveways in front of the building. The sidewalk curved around next to the driveway, leading right and left to big double doors at its apex—obviously the main entrance. There were about a thousand buses parked there and kids were spewing out of all of them.

"Whoa!" Ross said, looking out but not moving.

"Yeah," I said, also not moving.

Then Pete and that Lindsay girl and another girl, who turned out to be Lindsay's friend Hannah, came back down the bus aisle to where we were, and Pete said, "Let's go, buddy," to me, and Lindsay said, "It's not as bad as it looks. Come on—let's find your homeroom. You a freshman, too?" she asked Ross as me and Ross stood up. Ross and I. Whatever.

Ross nodded and we all got off and joined the crowd trying to fit through the double doors.

◇ ⬡ ◇

The first thing that hit me was the subway-rush-hour mob inside, kids all over the place, pushing and shoving and yelling and going in what seemed like all directions. I guess it hit Ross, too, because he stopped just inside the door and said, "Whoa! I didn't know there were so many people in Greenford, let alone so many kids!"

Lindsay gave him a smile and said, "I know, it's kind of overwhelming at first. But you get used to it. Come on. We'd better get you to the office."

Lindsay shepherded the three of us newbies through the crowd. She was really good at it. So was Pete, actually, but Ross and I kept bumping into kids and being bumped into, and then Ross started saying "sorry—pardon me—excuse me" over and over like it was a poem, and bowing and bobbing up and down. That cracked me up and I started doing the same thing. Pete turned around, and then he rolled his eyes at Lindsay and said, "I don't know these two, do you?" and she laughed and said, "I'm not sure— they do look a little familiar." And then the wall we were going along turned into this huge glass window with lots of desks behind it and women shuffling papers and looking harassed. The Office.

Lindsay pushed us inside, calling, "Hi, Mrs. Sanders" to the woman at the first desk, who looked old enough to be somebody's grandmother except for all the lipstick and stuff she had on her face.

"Lindsay Maller, as I live and breathe!" Mrs. Sanders said. "How was your summer?"

"Okay," Lindsay said. "How was yours?"

"Pretty good. A couple of weeks on the Cape was the highlight. What can I do for you?"

"I've got two new kids here, needing schedules and stuff. And another who doesn't know his way around yet."

"Welcome to GHS," Mrs. Sanders said, smiling

at the three of us, and then she asked our names and grubbed around on her desk till she found cards with Pete's and my homeroom numbers and schedules on them.

"I've got room one twenty-seven," Ross said, pulling a schedule out of his pocket that I guess he got over the summer. "What've you got?"

"One twenty-seven," I told him.

"Cool," Ross said as we left the office. Ross and I shoved through the crowd behind Lindsay and Peter till Lindsay pointed us at a half-open door with ROOM 127 painted on its frosted-glass window.

"Here's your room," she said. "Good luck, you guys." And she and Peter disappeared.

Gonna be better, gonna be better here, I found myself saying in my mind even though I didn't want to, as Ross and I went inside. We just stood there near the door, staring at the kids bustling around the room. There was no teacher in sight, and the kids were all shrieking hellos like they hadn't seen one another in decades. Pretty soon a really big guy with lots of black hair tied in a ponytail came up to Ross and sort of nodded at him and said, "Yeah, Terrel. You're back, huh?" which seemed to me pretty obvious, but what did I know? Maybe Ross was absent all last year from the middle school everyone in the room obviously went to.

"Yeah, Fitz, looks like. Listen, I got that new game, X-Q Killers. It's really cool."

Fitz said, "Yeah? I got it, too," and he and Ross elbowed their way over to a bunch of other kids. I was still standing in the same place when the teacher came in.

She was kind of tall and thin and looked scared, like maybe she was new. Maybe it was her first year in high school, too, I figured. Turned out it was her second, but I didn't know that then. She gave me a big smile and strode up to the desk in the front of the room like she owned it, and I saw she wasn't scared at all. It was just her natural weird expression.

"Okay, people," she said. "Find seats."

As I went to sit down, I noticed this girl with blond little-girl braids halfway down her back, and solemn blue eyes, and small, delicate hands that caressed the pack she put down on her desk as if it was made of, I don't know, silk and roses maybe. Most of the other girls had on jeans and little clingy tops that showed their bellies, but this one wore a short dark blue skirt and a loose-fitting white blouse, like a Catholic school uniform. I couldn't stop staring at her.

The teacher announced that her name—not the girl's; her own name—was Ms. Blanchard, and she said we'd go to all our classes today but they'd be shorter than usual, and the first thing was going to be an assembly and would we all line up to go to it. When we lined up like good little freshmen, Ross came up to me and said that Fitz was kind of a jerk and not a real friend, and I asked him what that girl's name was, and he said, "Daisy. Cute, huh?"

I just nodded. I'd never had a girlfriend, even though there'd been girls I'd sort of had my eye on. But I'd never gotten up the nerve to talk to them after maybe sixth grade or so. This girl, though, this Daisy—well, I thought things sure *would* be better here if I could get to know her!

Then we went out into the hall again and lost the rest of our lined-up homeroom people in the mob that kind of took us along with them to the auditorium, like Ross and I were a couple of sticks someone had thrown into a fast-running river.

The auditorium was big, like a theater with seats going downhill to a real stage instead of just a gym with a platform at one end and chairs set up in it. This guy who turned out to be the principal was standing on the stage just sort of watching while we all poured in and sat down.

Finally he held up his hand and said in this really loud voice, "Welcome to GHS, new students, and welcome back, old students. So, how about it? Is this going to be the best year ever?"

A whole bunch of kids cheered, and Ross and I just looked at each other, like whoa, what was that about?

When the cheers died down, the principal gave this really boring speech and then made a lot of announcements about extracurricular activities, mostly sports. That involved a parade of jocks, with a humongous cheer for the varsity football team and its captain, who was supposed to be a real hero and the first junior ever to be captain. Big deal, right? The guy had a really weird name, but instead of using it like the principal did, the kids all chanted "Zorro, Zorro!" at him, and he grinned, so I figured that was what he went by.

One of the activities the principal listed was band, and I thought if they needed a drummer, maybe I could get into that. *Maybe there'll be other drummers, I* thought, *or other kids who write songs.* There was no mention of archery as a class or as an activity, though, and I tried to think one out of two wasn't bad—50 percent, you know? And by then I'd noticed there were a couple more cute girls in my homeroom besides Daisy, so I thought maybe I could even hook up with one of them pretty soon.

Then it was back to the river in the halls, and I said, "I'm a trout, glub, glub," to Ross and made swimming motions, and he cracked up like it was really funny. We both swam back to homeroom and then to lunch, and all our classes after that. At lunch we sat at a table with a couple of other guys—Fitz and this real quiet kid, Morris Something or Something Morris. Morris, anyway. He was kind of fat and had almost as many zits as me. After lunch, that Zorro kid from the assembly—you know, the football guy—and a couple of his buddies kind of stared at Ross and me as we swam by on our way to whatever class we had next, and that cracked us up more.

Yeah, well, that was pretty dumb, come to think of it, cracking up when we saw them.

Anyway, later . . .

FALCO: Whoops. Hold on a sec, Gray. Sorry. Have to change the tape. There's stuff on this one about the—er—incident, stuff before I added our interview . . . Sorry. The other tapes will last longer . . . There. Okay, later? . . .

Later, like that night when I was in my room and Barker and I were on my bed, I could see a couple of lights on upstairs in the Mallers' house next door. "So, Barker," I said, watching the lights and rubbing Barker's belly, "the good thing about first days of school probably pretty much everywhere is meaningless homework, and guess what? Mine's already done. It'll get harder, I bet, but maybe I can do homework every night here, what do you think?"

Barker licked my hand, which made his head go up and down, so I pretended that was a yes. But I knew I'd probably have to really work on getting my homework done every night instead of never, like at the end of the time in my old school.

"It wasn't much of a first day," I told Barker, "but, hey, nothing bad happened. Ten points for Greenford High!" So far, Greenford High seemed like any other school, except a whole lot bigger. I wondered how weird it was going to be to go to the same school as Peter. I'd figured I'd keep seeing him around corners and in the halls, but I hadn't seen him all day, and I was just as glad. "Pete won't spy, though, right?" I said to Barker, who brushed his tail against my quilt. "Yeah, he won't," I said.

But still, I thought Pete's being around would make me feel kind of like I was being watched, like Dad had been watching me at home to make sure I didn't slip and do something I shouldn't.

Okay, see, I knew that was really why we'd moved. I knew Dad had started looking for a job as soon as stupid Parker Middle School had suspended me the second time, even though it was only bad luck I'd been caught with the knife on me. Hell, Bruce Tolliver had a knife, and Hank Angelo; they'd had theirs by the time they were halfway through seventh grade at Parker. What Dad never got, even back when I was in elementary school and kids pestered me, was that a lot of the time if guys like them knew you could fight back, you'd be safe. But if you didn't show them that, which by middle school—my middle school, anyway—meant if you didn't carry something, like as not you'd be dead meat. Even Jemmy had a chain he kept in his pocket, not a sink-stopper-type chain, either.

Anyway, The Suspensions. It's not like I'd used the knife, just pulled it when Bruce and Hank cornered me one too many times, whispering "wuss" and "fag" and mincing around in circles, flapping their hands and laughing because Mr. Franklin had kept me after school to tutor me in social studies, which I sure as hell hadn't asked him to do. Everyone knew about Mr. Franklin, but that didn't mean I was like that. "Takes one to know one," Bruce had said. "Sweetie."

I got mad, like anger was a wave breaking over me, and my hand reached for the knife before I told it to, and then it pulled it out.

The knife shut them up pretty quick, too.

It was just my luck the principal came along right after I'd pulled it. And just my luck, too, that he didn't understand any better than Dad did about weapons. Suspension Number One.

In the middle of me thinking about all that, Barker whimpered and twitched like he was remembering it, too. Yeah, maybe he was, for I sure told him about it back when it happened, like I told him everything. Anyway, now I patted him and looked out the window again.

One of the lights in the Mallers' house had gone off, but the other one was still on. Which window is Linda—no, Lindsay's—I wondered.

The second suspension was really stupid, stupid on my part. I felt myself wince, remembering how dumb I'd been. Okay, so it's hard to move a drum set around, especially in Parker Middle School's tiny gym, but I was really, really dumb to bend down so far to maneuver my bass that the damn knife fell out of my pocket. Come to think of it, it was also dumb to even still have the knife by then, since Bruce and Hank had been pretty quiet for a while.

Yeah, but quiet like they were planning something. Just waiting. Biding their time.

The way I am here, I thought. Here in Greenford where there don't seem to be any green Fords. Doesn't seem right, somehow. The Fords, I mean.

Gonna be better, gonna be better here.

Maybe, I thought, *Dad will even stop getting on my case.* It wasn't as if he and I had ever really been able to talk about much of anything, but I'd always thought he was an okay guy and he'd always seemed to like me well enough. Okay, maybe he didn't feel about me the way he did about Peter, but Peter'd always taken after him more than me anyway, so why wouldn't Dad like him better? And of course Peter never made mistakes, at least not that anyone knew about. Perfect Peter.

Ever since Suspension Number Two, though, it had been like Dad was afraid I'd do something really terrible if he didn't watch me all the time and lecture me and stuff. Creepy, you know? My own father. He and Mom had this big fight before we moved, because the principal at Parker wanted me to go to some kind of counseling, and Mom wanted me to do it, but Dad didn't. I just stood there listening to him yell, and it sounded like he thought I wasn't even human—like I was this *thing* that he had to dispose of so it wouldn't bother him or embarrass him or whatever anymore.

FALCO: How did that make you feel?

GRAY: How do you think? Like shit, that's how.

FALCO: Yes, but what did that feel like inside? Mad? Hurt? Lonely?

GRAY: I don't know. Maybe all of them? I don't know!

FALCO: So what did your dad decide?

GRAY: Not much . . .

He said he could take care of whatever problems I had, and he didn't want anyone else interfering. And of course he won, like he always does.

Yeah, well, I didn't want anyone interfering, either. Especially not him. His way of taking care of problems is mostly to yell.

All I wanted to do in Greenford, Connecticut, was play my drums and get through high school.

Yeah, I wanted to work on my songs and my drums and, okay, my homework, and think about what I was gonna do with my life so I wouldn't end up a nothing, you know, a blank like some people and like I'd been so far except for music and archery. *There's gotta be a reason why I'm here,* I kept thinking. "All I've got to do is find out what it is," I said to Barker.

Barker wagged his tail, so I gave him a pat.

One good thing about being in Greenford, I decided, was no one knew me; I could be whoever I wanted. No one knew about Mr. Franklin tutoring me; no one knew about Bruce and Hank; no one knew about the knife. So I could start again. They'd even told me at Parker that they don't send behavior-type records on to kids' high schools. Everyone gets to start with a "clean slate." So things would *have* to be better. Better in Greenford.

I went over the day again in my mind.

That guy Ross had seemed okay. No Jemmy, maybe, but okay. See, Jemmy was really cool. He could do stuff I couldn't, like hit home runs and talk to girls, but he never got on my case about what I couldn't do. He always cheered for me in archery, and he cheered for me even when we did stuff in PE that I wasn't good at. When we were maybe in, like, third grade, he and I invented a hide-and-seek game with Barker. We used to play that for hours, and once we played it in the woods and got lost, which made Mom worried and Dad mad. But Jemmy covered for me. He said it was his fault. He always covered for me when I needed a cover, and I always covered for him. He always laughed at my jokes, too.

Well, most of them, anyway.

I wasn't sure that Ross or anyone else would turn out to be like that, but Jemmy and I were going to keep in touch and he was going to come visit, maybe sometime during summer vacation.

Meanwhile, it looked like there was Ross, and there was Daisy, too—another plus, maybe. And the computers at the school media center looked pretty good; Ross and I had checked them out for a few minutes after dismissal. "I've got a better one at home," Ross told me. "And a bunch of cool games. You could come over sometime, maybe, if you want."

Thinking about all that made me want to call

Jemmy. But when I looked at my watch, I saw it was too late.

Shit, I thought.

Soon the other light at the Mallers' went out, making everything dark except for a dim streetlight halfway down the block, and the glow of a couple of TV sets.

Not quite a black hole out there in Greenford, Connecticut.

"Maybe that's a good sign," I told Barker.

I figured I might as well go to bed.

FALCO: Good, Gray! Okay. So you met Ross and liked him. And you'd seen that girl . . .

GRAY: Daisy.

FALCO: Right. Daisy. And a couple of other girls, and those other guys at your lunch table. Sounds like a pretty good start. Who else? Who else did you meet at school? What about that football guy, that Zorro?

GRAY: Yeah. Zorro . . .

See, it turned out there were Bruces and Hanks in Greenford, too. It sure didn't take them long to find Ross and me. We had PE last period, right before varsity football practice. I guess it was the second day that we had it out on the football field.

"Okay, guys," yelled Mr. Vee; he was our PE teacher as well as the varsity football coach. "Let's start with passing. Team up with the guy next to you and pass back and forth." He tossed balls at us, and Fitz, that guy with the ponytail we'd had lunch with the first day, caught one and lobbed it at me and of course I dropped it. Football's not my sport, you know? It turned out it wasn't Ross's, either; he didn't even come close to catching the ball some other guy threw to him.

"Jeez," Fitz said, looking around at Ross. "You still suck, Terrel, you know?"

"Yeah," Ross said, "but that other guy can't throw."

We went on like that for a while, with me and Ross being pretty spastic, and finally Mr. Vee paired us together so he could concentrate on the kids who were good or almost good, and told us to practice passing. Right away Ross and me started kidding around—it was actually even fun for a while. I remember Ross tossed the ball under his arm to me, and I tossed it over my shoulder, backward, to him, and then he tried to make it spin on its end, and I grabbed it and tried to make it spin on my head.

By then we were both cracking up, and Ross was laughing so hard he was kind of wobbly. I lifted up my leg and threw the ball under it, sort of a variation on that counting thing little girls do bouncing a ball, and Ross tried to kick it, but he fell sprawling on the ground instead.

Somewhere during all this the varsity guys, who had paraded out onto the field earlier like they'd paraded across the stage at assembly the first day, started watching us.

I didn't even know they were there till one of them—the captain, the guy from the assembly who everyone called Zorro—shouted, "Hey, Mr. Vee, how come you've got a couple of girls in your freshman class this year?"

Ross started looking around like he really thought there were girls there, but I knew right away who and what the guy meant, and I got the same feeling in my stomach I used to get with Bruce and Hank back at Parker Middle School.

Mr. Vee just sort of grinned and said, "Lay off, guys, not everyone's a star," and went back to coaching this huge kid who looked like he was already a professional linebacker or something.

But the varsity guys weren't about to lay off. As soon as Mr. Vee had his back turned, they came over to us, sauntering in that side-to-side way guys like them have, almost like they're on a ship and think they have to put all their weight on one foot and then on the other to keep their balance. They stood there watching us and grinning.

Ross tossed the ball to me sort of uncertainly, and I fumbled it, but I picked it up real quick. Then I held on to it and tried to stare the varsity guys off.

"It's okay, girlie," Zorro said, snickering. "Don't mind us. We'll just watch you play catch with your girlfriend."

The other guys laughed and poked each other.

"We're done," I said, and started to walk off the field, figuring that if we just faded away, they'd stop and maybe that'd be it, the end, no more, no Parker School replay.

"Oh, no, you're not." Another guy grabbed me. "We like to watch girls play. Go ahead." He shoved me away from him. "Throw it—faggot."

"Ooooo!" Zorro shrieked in this weird squeaky voice his pals thought was hysterical. "Yeah, you go, *girl*!"

Well, okay, sorry, but that did it. I pulled my arm back and instead of aiming at Ross, I aimed the ball at the first guy who'd grabbed me, hoping to hit him with it, hard, but of course he caught it. "No, this way!" he said, and he shot it hard at Ross. The ball hit Ross in the stomach. His baseball cap fell off, and I could hear the breath being knocked out of him as he doubled over.

The varsity guys laughed and so did everyone in our class, all of whom were watching by then. I could feel my stomach churning and my fists balling up, and by then I was sure as heck wishing I had my knife, except there were too many of them for me to be able to use it. Plus the coach was there.

Mr. Vee finally turned away from the big lunk he was talking to and said mildly to the varsity kids, "You fellas better go get changed for practice."

"This guy threw right *at* him," I yelled to Mr. Vee, going over to Ross and picking up his cap. He was still gasping and looking as if he was going to hurl.

"Mistake, man," the guy who'd thrown at him called over his shoulder as he and his pals sauntered off.

"Football's a rough sport," was all Mr. Vee said to Ross. "Build up your abs, and you'll be able to take it better." Then he blew his whistle and made us do laps around the field for a while till class was over.

FALCO: That sure can't have been much help. What about you and Ross? Did you just take it—put up with it, or what?

GRAY: Yeah, sort of, for a while, I guess. On the outside, anyway. Not that we wanted to. At least I sure didn't . . .

The rest of that day, I kept thinking about it and about how those varsity guys were as bad as Bruce and Hank at Parker and a heck of a lot bigger. And later that night, I dug my knife out of the bottom of this box in my closet where I kept old comics and stuff that Mom never looked at when she cleaned. I put it on the table next to my bed and stared at it for a while.

"What do you think, Barker?" I asked him. "Should I carry it again?"

Barker thumped his tail.

I picked up the knife and ran my thumb along the edge of the blade. It was still pretty sharp. Then I hefted it in my hand. It made my hand feel good, sort of strong and firm.

But then I thought about the suspensions, and Dad being so mad, and about how everything was gonna change in Greenford, and I put the knife back on the table and lay down.

Barker jumped up beside me and put his head on my chest like he often did, and I played with his ears and listened to him make happy grunting noises for a while. But it was like there was this movie in my head of Bruce and Hank and the varsity guys and the stuff all of them said, and I could feel myself getting mad again.

Maybe scared, too, some.

"I'm no fag," I whispered to Barker. "Or wuss or loser or any of the other things. Right, Barker?"

Barker gave me a big slobbery dog kiss and whined like he always did when he wanted to say something. I told myself he was agreeing with me and that maybe I could put the knife back in the box after all.

But then that movie played itself in my head again and I knew I was going to take the knife to school, hiding it somehow. No one would know unless I used it, and I promised myself I wouldn't use it unless I really had to—you know, if nothing really did change in Greenford. See, I was still giving it a chance to change.

"Just in case," I said to Barker. "Just in case."

FALCO: Mmm. What about Ross? Did you tell him about the knife?

GRAY: Not right away. I started carrying it the next day, though, in my sock. But I didn't say anything to Ross till maybe a week later, when we had another run-in with the varsity guys . . .

When Ross and I got off the bus, Zorro and his friends were on the front steps of the school and Zorro said, "Hey, look! Here are the girls!" They did some pretty fancy wolf whistling as we passed and one of them knocked Ross's cap off his head and the guys tossed it around.

So much for my "gonna change" mantra, I thought.

That afternoon I went to Ross's house. He lived in that really fancy neighborhood at the end of the bus route. The houses were big and they had big yards with lots of neatly mowed grass and bushes and flowers and stuff, and the houses were all different. Ross's was white with clapboards, I think they're called, those skinny horizontal boards that sort of overlap. And it had dark green shutters on the windows and a dark green door. It was pretty nice.

Ross's mom was nice, too. She called, "In the kitchen," as soon as Ross and I came in, and Ross said, "Come on," and led me down this hall off one side of which I could see was a fancy living room that looked as if no one ever lived in it. Off the other side was an even fancier dining room with one of those— what is it?—crystal-chandelier things hanging over a polished table. But there was a pair of dirty sneakers under the table and a pile of what looked like mail on it, so that room looked a little more used. Later I found out it really was, too, because I actually ate with them in it.

The kitchen was big and sunny and painted yellow, and I remember thinking Mom would love it, because she'd always said she wanted a yellow kitchen. Ours in Massachusetts had been dark and small with grungy striped wallpaper, and ours in Greenford was bigger but green instead of yellow. Mom said it was boring and like everyone else's in what she called "the subdivision," but maybe we could paint it someday. Dad hadn't seemed exactly eager, though, and I figured we never would.

Anyway, Mrs. Terrel was what Grandma would have called "pleasingly plump," and she had brown curly hair around the top and sides of her round face like it was a close-fitting hood. Her face was red, too, and she was holding a full cookie sheet.

"You're just in time, boys," she said, putting the cookies down. "Who's this, Ross?"

"Gray Wilton," Ross said, reaching for a cookie, but his mom gave his hand a little flick with her finger. She seemed a lot more relaxed than my mom.

"Hi, Gray," she said. "The cookies have to cool a bit, but I'll bring some up when they're ready. Have some milk or something if you want." She got out a couple of glasses and opened the fridge. Ross and I grabbed sodas and went up this big curvy staircase to his room, me thinking, *Whoa, his family must really be rich!* But nice-rich, you know?

Later his mom brought a big plate of cookies up to us.

Ross's room was way bigger than mine, with a big desk and also a table with a couple of half-built model planes on it. Instead of posters, he had postcards all over his walls of places like Paris, France, and Nairobi, Kenya, which was kind of weird but nice, and he had this huge stack of CDs, even one of Third Wheel, which not too many people like, unless they're really into drums.

I picked it up and said, "Cool band—the best, you know?" kind of experimenting to see what he'd say.

"Yeah," he said, "they're okay, but I like Jakefish better."

I thought Jakefish was pretty old and their drummer was sort of spastic, but by then Ross had sat down at this truly awesome computer, which was on his desk.

"This game is the best," he said, sliding in a CD, and right away the screen was filled with this sort of school-looking building. Ross reached behind himself, pulled another chair up, and motioned me to sit, which I did. Then he took us in through the door of the building on the screen and along these dark corridors and suddenly this alien-looking guy popped out of a room.

"*BLAM!* Got him!" Ross yelled, zapping the alien.

Fire had flashed from the gun that showed at the front of Ross's computer screen. It was angled toward him like he was holding it. The alien fell, blood spurting from its chest.

"Your turn. Just aim and—yes! Man, you're good! Are you sure you've never done this before?"

"Sure." I grinned, grateful to archery, and shot down two more aliens. They made choking noises— *"Arrrr-urg!"*—as they fell.

"Watch." Ross moved farther along the virtual corridor, stalking invaders, and waited to shoot till an enemy scout was at point-blank range. Its cry ended abruptly as its brains splattered all over the walls. "He's the guy that threw the football at me," Ross said, so I knew he'd been thinking about that, too.

"Cool!" I ignored what my stomach was doing and took aim. "Here goes his buddy Zorro," I said, and I shot the next one. "And"—I offed two more— "here go Bruce and Hank."

Ross turned around, facing me. "Who're they?"

"Guys I used to know."

"They mess with you?"

"Yeah, kind of. But not after I showed them my knife."

"You carry a knife? Like, all the time?"

"You better believe it." I pulled it out of my sock.

His eyes got kind of big and he let out this long, one-note whistle.

I put it back in my sock and said, "Better safe than sorry, right?"

"I guess," Ross said slowly. "But it might be kind

of risky, having it on you at school. We've got this zero-tolerance thing in Greenford, you know? No weapons, no drugs."

"Yeah, well, I didn't see any metal detectors or cops or security guards, so how's anyone to find out? Besides, I won't use it unless I really have to."

Ross turned away and shot another alien.

◇ ◇ ◇

After that, I kept running into Zorro in the halls, and in the locker room between PE class and varsity football practice. He always kind of stared at me, and a few times he made a face at me—stuck his tongue out or screwed his face up like he'd smelled something bad. And then on this one day, he and this guy Johnson cornered me and Ross between two rows of lockers and kept pushing us and keeping us from leaving and yelling stuff at us like "Camouflage Girl" at Ross—I guess because of his camouflage jacket— and "Crater Face" at me, because of the zits, I guess. They thought it was really funny.

We didn't.

I sort of wanted to show them the knife then, but I couldn't get to it with them shoving us, and finally they gave us one last push and left.

The thing that bothered me, though, a lot, was

why? Why did they keep going after us? I didn't think it could just be the jacket and the zits.

Could it?

What was it about us? About me?

We hadn't done anything to those guys, like I hadn't done anything to Hank and Bruce at Parker Middle, either, nothing except be tutored by Mr. Fag—er, Franklin. But nothing like that had happened in Greenford. Sure, I was small and had zits, but hell, lots of kids are like that. And Ross was kind of weird, but so are other kids. So why pick on us?

Ross told me he got picked on in middle school, too. He said he tried to fight back and that didn't work, so he just sort of took it. Just sort of let them do it. But that didn't work, either, because it didn't stop.

I really wished I knew why. I guess I thought if I knew why, maybe I could figure out how to stop it.

FALCO: Right. Makes sense. And we'll come back to that, but let's leave school for a minute. It says something about a youth group in the file they gave me about you. Was that . . .

GRAY: What file? Who gave it to you?

FALCO: The police . . . Gray?

GRAY: Yeah, what?

FALCO: They interviewed some people after—you
    know.

GRAY: Figures.

FALCO: Okay, tell me about the youth group. Was
    that the one at that church your folks went to?
    Good Shepherd?

GRAY: Yeah.

FALCO: And? . . . You went with your brother the
    first time, right? . . . Gray? Come on. I need you
    to talk to me.

GRAY: Yeah, but this is getting kind of boring, you
    know? So thanks, but no thanks. Like, sorry, but
    I don't need to talk to you!

FALCO: I think you do. But okay, maybe not right
    now. I'll be back tomorrow. We'll talk more then.

FALCO: Hi, Gray. Feeling any better today?

GRAY: Mr. Falco?

FALCO: Yes?

GRAY: Is this really going to help? Telling you about
    it?

FALCO: Yes, son, it is. I need to know as much as
    possible about you, about how you felt and still
    feel, and about what happened. The more I
    know, the better I'll be able to help you, to
    defend you . . . Okay?

GRAY: Ummm. Shit . . . Yeah. I guess. Maybe.

FALCO: Okay. Now—the youth group. The first time
   you went. Start with something easy, like, I
   don't know, the weather.
GRAY: The *weather?* Jeez! . . .

Well, I remember it was pouring rain the first time
Pete went, and Mom made me go, too.

I was in a crummy mood because I'd asked Dad
for the hundredth time to let me play my drums
without practice pads on them muting the sound,
but he'd said no for the hundredth time, because he
was afraid of bothering our new neighbors. He kept
saying the cellar wasn't soundproofed and that was
where I had to practice, and yes, he'd ask the neighbors if we could work out a special time, but not till
we knew them better. He'd said all that before and
he still hadn't done anything about asking them. The
thing is, I'd been thinking about a new song, but I
knew I couldn't get the drum part right, or the
whole thing, really, with the damn practice pads.

So I was pretty pissed when Pete and I left for
youth group.

It was raining so hard we could hardly see out the
windshield even with the wipers on at top speed.
And even with rain jackets—Mom made us wear
them—we were pretty soaked when we got to the
parish house, which wasn't really a house but a wing

attached to the church. A girl told us to hang our jackets on this rack in the hall where they could drip, and then she pointed to a room where there were sofas and armchairs—sort of like a living room but lined up in semicircular rows—and a big table with a white cloth and candles on it in the front and a fireplace behind that. I thought maybe there was going to be some kind of church service because of the table, but there wasn't.

Kids kept coming in and hugging each other and saying hi, kind of like at school that first day but a lot quieter. Then in a couple of minutes Lindsay Maller came in and Peter beckoned to her and she sat down next to him. They started talking, but then some guy got up and said his name was Dick Cathrell and he was the president of the group. I tuned out when he read through a list of stuff the group was going to do that year, but I tuned in again when he said, "Okay, time for introductions. We've got four new freshmen"—I looked around but I didn't see anyone I recognized, especially not Ross—"and a new senior. The senior's the brother of one of the freshmen, actually, so let's start with them."

I tried being invisible again.

"Could you stand up, please," Dick Cathrell said, "when I introduce you? Maybe you could tell us a little about yourselves, too. Everyone, this is Peter Wilton and his brother, Gray Wilton. Welcome, guys!"

Everyone clapped when Peter stood up, like he'd already done something wonderful, and he yanked me up, too, so there went my invisibility.

"You guys are from Massachusetts, right?" Dick prompted.

"That's right," Peter said. "Small city of East Hamilton. It's kind of an old mill town, actually, but fixed up. Our dad got a new job, in New York, so we came here. Kind of a long commute from Massachusetts, you know?"

There was a ripple of polite laughter, and of course some of the girls leaned out of their seats to get a better look at Peter.

"So, Peter," said Dick, "tell us about yourself. What makes you tick?"

Peter grinned. "Wine, women, and song?" Everyone except me laughed again, Peter included. "No, not really. Let's see. I'm a senior, like Dick said, at Greenford High, which I guess is where most of you go, since it looks like it's the only show in town, and I like basketball and baseball, and science and history. I'll be doing premed in college, so I'm kind of what people call a serious student—some of the time." He turned to me. "You're next, buddy."

"Nah, that's okay," I think I said. I felt my face getting red, so I looked down. "Nothing to say."

"Oh, come on, Gray." Dick Cathrell came over and gave me what I guess he thought was a friendly pat on the back. "No one's marking this, man; it's not a test. We just want to know who you are."

I looked up. *Okay,* I thought. *I'll give it to them.* "Who I am?" I said in a loud voice. "Nobody, I guess." Once I'd said it, it sounded weirder than I'd meant and not at all funny, which *is* what I'd meant. Sort of, anyway. Afterward, I wished I hadn't said it, but you can't take back words, and I knew if I tried to, I'd mess up worse, so I just sat down.

A couple of kids laughed in an embarrassed way and Pete put his arm across my shoulders, which made it even *more* worse, if that was possible. "Gray's too modest," he said. "He's just about the best shot with a bow I've ever seen, and he's not bad with a shotgun, either—I forgot to say we go hunting with our dad. And he's a real cool songwriter and drummer, much to our folks' dismay."

I guess he was trying to be nice, but I was too embarrassed to deal with it, and missing my drums too much to want to be reminded of them. I managed to mutter to him, "Thanks, but could you just shut up about me?"

We sat down and Dick introduced the other freshmen. I knew for sure then that they weren't in any of my classes, and I was just as glad since I'd made such a jerk of myself. After that there were committee reports and assignments, and Lindsay and Peter both got on the same committee, something to do with what they called the winter retreat, like they were an army going backward in the snow. It turned out that they were all going to go someplace in the country for a weekend, to think about God or Life or something. Then there were refreshments, which some of the girls put on the table in the front of the room, the one with the candles on it. A couple of kids came over and said hi and I said hi back, and one of the freshmen said he thought he'd seen me around, but I hadn't seen him, so that was the end of that.

Finally it was over and I waited in the car while Peter stood outside in the rain talking to Lindsay till her mother came and picked her up.

FALCO: Thank you, Gray. That was helpful. Hey, I think I just learned something important about you!
GRAY: Yeah, what?
FALCO: You like being funny, right? Making people laugh?

GRAY: Do I?

FALCO: Don't you?

GRAY: Yeah. Yeah, I guess. But I mess up a lot when I try it, and then it's not so funny, you know?

FALCO: I do. There's nothing more embarrassing than a joke that falls flat.

GRAY: Yeah, it's like the guy telling the joke falls flat. I mean really falls down, you know?

FALCO: Right.

GRAY: You're laughing. A little.

FALCO: Yup. Because that *was* funny. Maybe not wildly funny, but funny . . . We'd better get back to work. Did you and Peter go back to the youth group?

GRAY: Peter did. Not me. I guess I'm not much of a group player.

FALCO: What about church?

GRAY: Yeah, we all went to church. Every Sunday, just about.

FALCO: What did you think of it?

GRAY: Think of it? Not much. It seemed hypocritical, you know? At least for me. I didn't know if I believed what the rest of them believed, about God and stuff. So I didn't really belong. I used to sit there and write songs in my head. I didn't belong there any more than I did at school, I guess.

FALCO: Let's go back to that. How did it go, you
    know, how was it going at school by, say, the
    end of September?

Well, by then I knew I'd sure been right about nothing changing, even though I still kept wanting it to.
It got to be a sort of routine—Zorro and the other
varsity guys—kind of a repeat of the stuff at Parker
School. Shit, I was mad, but what could I do? For
a while it seemed like trying to ignore it might be
the safest thing to do, instead of pulling the knife
on them. I sure didn't want to get suspended again.
And I wasn't sure anymore the knife would do
much good. But the whole thing was weird because
a couple of times the varsity guys had said stuff to
Fitz and Morris, the silent guys Ross and I ate
with. . . .

FALCO: Silent guys?
GRAY: Yeah, they didn't talk much. It was like we
    had the weird table at lunch, you know? None
    of us fit anyplace else so we ate together, but we
    weren't really friends, except for me and Ross.
    Fitz sometimes talked a little, but hey, what he
    was into was bugs! Like once he brought this
    cockroach to lunch, and that really grossed me
    out. I mean, it was funny, but it was lunch, you

know? And Morris was kind of a brain; he used
to read a lot at lunch.

FALCO: When I was in eighth grade, we used to have
ant races . . .

GRAY: Yeah?

FALCO: Yeah. So anyway, what did Fitz and Morris
do about the varsity guys?

GRAY: Nothing. That was the weird thing . . .

Fitz and Morris just laughed it off and after a while
the varsity guys left them alone, so we thought, me
and Ross, that if we laughed it off, maybe they'd leave
us alone, too. But it didn't work. It's like they thought
we were different. Maybe they knew it got to us
more than it got to Fitz and Morris. I don't know.

FALCO: Maybe. So it did get to you more?

GRAY: I guess.

FALCO: In what way?

GRAY: Man, I don't know! It just did. Maybe because
of the stuff back at Parker. But I don't know
about Ross. Maybe because he'd had trouble
before, too. Can we talk about something else?

FALCO: Sure. What about classes? How were you
doing in them, I mean academically?

GRAY: Okay. I was really trying to keep up, you
know, do homework and stuff . . .

I had this kind of neat guy for math, Mr. Wallace. If I had a favorite subject besides music, math was it, and so far I'd done okay in it. I guess English was my worst subject, and we had this teacher who really liked grammar, which I hated, so I wasn't doing so well in that. I used to play a game in my head about which punctuation mark she looked like each day, and then when I ran out of punctuation marks, I did math symbols and then music symbols and stuff. Most of the time she was forte, but I remember this one day she was pianissimo. The next day, she wasn't there and the principal announced her mom had died or something.

FALCO: How did you feel about that?

GRAY: About her mom dying? I don't know. Sorry for her, I guess. I mean that's hard, but she wasn't a kid, you know? She was pretty old. It would be worse for a kid's mom to die.

FALCO: How about your mom? How would you feel if she died?

GRAY: Shit, man! I'd be sad. Who wouldn't be if their mom died?

FALCO: How would a mom feel if her kid died? . . . Gray? . . . Hey, come on back here!

GRAY: Sad, damnit, okay? Anyway, about stuff at school . . .

One day at the end of September, Ross and me were in the locker room after PE, trying to figure out this weird math problem. The other guys in our class had left and it was still too early for the varsity guys to come in. We'd just about figured the problem out and were going to leave, when guess what? In came Zorro and Johnson, strutting like they owned the place, and when they looked at us and then at each other and grinned, my stomach just about shriveled up like a raisin.

"Well, well, well," Johnson said.

Zorro shook his head. "Not well," he said in this mournful voice. "Not well at all. Looks like we got us a couple of trespassers."

"We were just leaving." Ross reached for the math book, but Johnson shot his arm out at him and there was this huge metallic bang as Johnson slammed Ross against the nearest locker.

My tiny shriveled raisin stomach just about dropped to the floor.

"Looks like we got some educating to do," Zorro said. He grabbed my shoulders. "This locker room," he said, pushing me slowly backward toward the lockers, "belongs to us. We let other guys—"

"—lesser guys," Johnson said.

"—lesser guys—use it as long as they treat it with

respect. This is a *locker* room, you little turds, not the library. You come in, you change, you go to class; you come back and shower and get dressed. And"— he gave my shoulders a shake—"you leave. You little turds have to learn some respect."

"Yeah," Johnson echoed, giving Ross another shove. "Obviously, Z, these children haven't yet figured out that varsity rules. Or maybe they're just too dumb."

"Well, but they need to learn that, don't they? Even dumb little turds can learn a *little* respect." He'd gotten me to the bank of lockers now, and he gave me a shove against them. I felt a sharp handle bite into my back, and I bit my tongue, trying not to let him know it hurt.

"A lot of respect," Johnson said, giving Ross a shake.

Out of the corner of my eye, I saw a few other varsity types coming in. They grinned and poked each other and then settled down to watch the show, laughing.

"You gotta learn to look up to varsity, Crater Face," Zorro said. "You learn that"—he glanced over at Ross—"you and your bud here, you'll get along just fine. Varsity rules! Now you say it: Varsity rules."

What else could I do? I didn't want to, but there was no way I was dumb enough to refuse. "Varsity rules," I said, sort of spitting it at him.

Johnson put his hand on Ross's chin and pushed his head back, saying, "Acknowledge, Camouflage Girl."

"Yeah, acknowledge," Zorro said, shaking me by the shoulders against the lockers. "Once more with feeling. Both of you."

"Varsity rules," we both said.

The other guys were still laughing like they were watching a comedy routine.

My throat was getting tight and I tried to keep swallowing to stop my stomach-raisin from swimming up to my mouth. I figured I was next in line for the head-pushing action, and my back really hurt where Zorro was banging me against the lockers. I looked over at Ross again and I didn't see how he could breathe with Johnson forcing his head back like he was doing, so I yelled, "Cut it out!" At the same time, Ross pulled his arm back like he was going to punch Johnson, but Johnson grabbed his arm and wrenched it back, and Johnson and Zorro both laughed. In a really high voice, Zorro squealed, "Oooh, it fights back now, does it?" and Johnson said, "Say 'Please, Mr. Johnson, let go of my arm.'"

Ross looked like he was biting his lips to keep

from saying it, but he finally did, and Johnson
let go.

◯ ◯ ◯

The next day, Ross went to Mr. Vee and told him
what those guys did. But all Mr. Vee said was, "Sticks
and stones, Mr. Terrel, sticks and stones." I guess
maybe Ross didn't tell him the whole story, but even
so, like names don't matter? Like they don't make
you feel really mad?

Still, Ross and I agreed we should go back to
ignoring the varsity guys, at least for a while, since
not ignoring them seemed to make it worse, at least
for us. Fitz and Morris seemed to be able to ignore
them, though. It was like Fitz and Morris didn't exist
for Zorro and company anymore. Maybe they
weren't as much fun to go after as me and Ross; I
don't know. I still kept wanting to blow up, but like
I said before, the varsity guys were a lot bigger than
us and there were a lot more of them.

And anyway, I had my knife. I was still carrying
it in my sock, which seemed to be the most incon-
spicuous place. I didn't want to use it, and I knew
maybe it wouldn't work if I did, but at least I had it
in case things really got bad.

There was one good thing, though, for a while—
or almost good thing—about Greenford High, and

that was music class and band. Math was okay, too, like I said, because it was easy and because I liked it and because Daisy was in my class. A few times in class I got to explain something that she didn't understand. When someone asked Mr. Wallace about something, he'd ask if anyone could explain it, and if it was Daisy who'd asked, I'd say yes. Daisy usually gave me a big smile when I'd finished and she'd gotten it.

Music class and band were the best, though. In them I felt, I don't know, like my real self, maybe? More than in math. Well, lots more. Mr. Halifax, the music teacher, was also band leader, and he really liked percussion. In class he even used to talk a little about music theory and composition and stuff, and I really dug that.

Back on the day we had band auditions, which was the day I met him, I got there early and started fooling around with this drum set the school had. It was kind of battered, and the heads needed tightening, so I was doing that when Mr. Halifax came in, and he said, "Hey, no one touches the instruments without permission!"

But he didn't sound mad, and right away he asked, "Who are you? Do you know about drums?"

So I told him, and then he told me that the head on the big bass kept loosening and he really needed to have the skin replaced but the band—bands, ac-

tually; there was marching band and concert band—
the bands didn't have much money. He let me fool
around a little without practice pads while he pretended to do something else, but he was really listening, because after a while he said, "You're really
good, you know that?"

"Yeah," I said.

"That was pretty cool, too, what you were doing."

"It's kind of the background for a song I've been
working on." I didn't add that I'd had to work on it
in my head and by beating my hands on my bed-
room walls because Dad wouldn't let me practice at
full volume.

"Working on?" He had his head tilted to one
side, looking at me through these thick glasses he always wore.

"Writing."

"You want to show it to me sometime when
you've finished it?" he said. "I'd be glad to see it. Or
hear it."

"Yeah, sure," I told him. I was feeling my heart
kind of speed up, and I knew I was grinning. No one
had ever said anything like that to me before.

Then the rest of the kids came in. Halifax divided
everyone up into instruments and had people wait
outside till their instrument was called. There were
about ten other kids who were drummers. One was

a real quiet junior who'd been in concert band for a couple of years. He had this little snare drum of his own, which is all he had, and we both tried out on the big drum set, and I got the job. I felt kind of bad taking over the big ones from him, so I went over to him and apologized.

"Hey," he said. "It's okay, you're better'n me." That was pretty nice, you know? So I was thinking maybe GHS—that's Greenford High—wasn't going to be all that bad.

Mr. Halifax let the snare drummer stay in band anyway. I wasn't sure how that would work, but after the general band audition, there was another one, to decide who was going to be in marching band and go to all the football games and who was going to be in concert band and play concerts and maybe be part of the orchestra. So we all had to walk around with our instruments—I just used a little snare drum, like the kid I told you about used. We had to walk around—march, really—and play at the same time. That kid I told you about? He was really good at it. He went first. Then I went. I was awful. I mean, I couldn't do both things at once, play and march, even though I was supposed to march to the beat I was playing. And then I tripped, like over my own feet, and went crashing down, and everyone laughed. Falling flat, you know, like my jokes. The drum rolled away from me and I grabbed for it, but I missed and I ended up sort of crawling after it, and everyone was laughing like they'd never stop. Finally Mr. Halifax grabbed the drum and pulled me up and glared at everyone. They went on laughing and pointing at me and saying things like "Have a nice trip?" and "Fall guy!" so I said, "Yeah, need to work on my foot-eye coordination," and then the laughing got to be at the joke. That one didn't fall flat.

FALCO: Good for you! Still, that must've been embarrassing at first.

GRAY: Yeah. But I guess it turned out okay.

FALCO: Thanks to you, Gray. Quick recovery. So anyway, what happened? I guess you didn't get into marching band? Did that other drummer? Did you and he become friends?

GRAY: No. He got in, but not me, and I hardly ever saw him after that. We had separate practices and he wasn't in any of my classes.

FALCO: But you did get into concert band, right?

GRAY: Right.

FALCO: So you at least had that at GHS. Music. Mr. Halifax.

GRAY: Yeah. For a while. But Dad still wouldn't let me practice at full volume, so I couldn't work

at home. I sure missed that old garage in
Massachusetts, you know?

FALCO: I bet you did! And we can come back to that.
Anything else about the first weeks or so of
school? Anything just for freshmen, some kind
of orientation or something?

GRAY: Oh, yeah, there was this assembly just
for us, run by the guidance counselor, Ms.
Throckmorton. What a name, right? Sounds like
something out of an old horror movie. She'd be
the mysterious—I don't know—widow lady in the
haunted house who turns out to be a witch. Or
maybe not a witch—she had bushy red hair,
which I guess witches don't have—maybe a
murderer. Revenge killer; maybe someone killed
her—her cat or something.

FALCO: Wow! Revenge murder!

GRAY: Yeah, well, whatever.

FALCO: If it was, do you think that would make it
okay? You know, because she was mad about
her cat? Or upset about it?

GRAY: Shit, you ask weird stuff! I don't know. I just
made it up. I'm not writing a book or anything.

FALCO: Maybe you could, though. Sounds to me like
you could be better in English than you think.
Did you ever write stuff like that down? Seems

to me you must've had some feelings like that.
You know, because of . . .

GRAY: Not really. No. Hell, all I meant was
Throckmorton's name was weird. No big deal!

FALCO: Okay. Right. So about that guidance
assembly? What was it like?

GRAY: Pretty lame . . .

We all got herded into the cafeteria, and they made us sit at the tables in the front and they passed out paper and pencil. Then Throckmorton stood up and welcomed us to the school and told us more about extracurricular activities and said if we had any problems, we should go to her, *blah, blah, blah.* The thing I remember most was that she talked about self-esteem, which means liking yourself. If you don't like yourself, she said, how can other people like you? She passed out paper and told us to make a list of five good things about ourselves, five things we liked. She said we didn't have to put our names on our papers so the lists would be confidential. Got a piece of paper? . . . Thanks. Here's my list.

1. ~~Drums~~
2. ~~Archery~~

I didn't get any further than one and two, and I decided to cross them out because even though *I* liked that I was good at them and thought they were good things, I knew my parents didn't—at least Dad didn't—so I figured maybe they didn't really count even though I thought they were good things about me. Either that, or Ms. Throckmorton's system was wrong. I thought of putting something down about Barker, because I knew he liked me and I liked that he did, and I thought liking a dog a lot had to be a good thing, but I really didn't know why I thought that or what to put, and besides, I was pretty sure dogs' opinions wouldn't count for Throckmorton's questions. Maybe they don't count at all, except maybe to people who have dogs.

FALCO: No, I guess they might not have counted with Ms. Throckmorton. But I think most people who like dogs think dogs have a pretty accurate opinion about who's a good person and who isn't—and as you said, Barker liked you a lot. But Ms. Throckmorton probably wanted *your* opinion about yourself . . . Okay, so how were things with your parents around that time? How were things going at home? You mentioned hunting. Did you and your brother and your dad ever go hunting that fall?

GRAY: Yeah. Yeah, we did . . .

"Bright October weather," Mom said cheerfully one morning at breakfast.

"Hunting weather." Dad winked at Peter.

I put down my milk glass, hoping that what was coming next wouldn't.

But it did.

"How about it, boys? Weatherman says it'll be clear this weekend. Get the old guns oiled and go get us some ducks. No blind, but thanks to my foresight, we're nice and legal."

My stomach did its usual thing; it stabbed me. See, Dad had made me and Pete take hunting courses back in Massachusetts as soon as each of us was old enough, and he'd had us apply for Connecticut licenses before we'd even moved. I realized they must've just come in the mail. I think I'd been hoping they'd get lost or be denied or something.

I glanced at Mom, who I knew was on my side about hunting. But I could see that, as usual, there was no way she was going to stand up to Dad.

"Sure, Dad," Peter said, enthusiastically, of course. "Great."

There was a pause while Mom silently passed out bacon and I tried to practice invisibility again. But I could feel myself getting mad.

That's another thing. Did I tell you I've got what my sixth-grade teacher in elementary school called "a temper problem"? "Grayson holds anger in," Mrs. Stebbins put on one of my report cards, "but when he's pushed, he tends to explode." At the time, I thought that was pretty cool: "Tends to explode."

Dad tended to do that, too. Peter didn't; that was one way he wasn't like Dad and I was. Pete was kind of a peacemaker, like Mom wanted to be. But she couldn't always pull it off, at least not with Dad, because mostly even when she started trying, all she ended up doing was giving in to him, which didn't solve anything or make things peaceful. We just all— what's the word—seethed? Yeah, seethed. It always kind of surprised me that Mom gave in. I mean, I don't think she was wimpy as a nurse. How could she be?

Anyway, Dad flipped a piece of bacon deftly into his mouth. "So, Gray," he said. "Time you went for bigger game, kid. You and Barker, get Mom a nice fat duck for supper, huh?"

"Yeah, well . . ." I sort of choked as my stomach lurched again. "Yeah, well, thanks, Dad, but I—me and Ross, we're going to do something Saturday." That was true, too, although we hadn't figured out what. Maybe more computer games at his house, maybe a movie if the one theater in Greenford was playing anything decent, maybe just hanging out. But something; we'd decided that.

"What?" Dad bellowed. "Stare at that computer screen of his, shooting at little purple Martians or whatever it is you shoot at, and getting a big behind from sitting on it all day? Why do that when you can shoot at real stuff, huh?"

"Sure!" I yelled. "Shoot at real dangerous little ducks, right, Dad? Real tough-guy stuff, right?"

"Gray, Harry," Mom pleaded. "Take it easy! Harry, maybe . . ."

"This is guy stuff, Samantha; you keep out of it," Dad shouted. "As for you, Gray, there sure isn't anything tough about computer games. If I have to drag you into the real world, so help me, I will!" He slurped his coffee, waved the cup, made his voice real calm, and said, "You bring Ross along, Gray. Tell him your old man says there aren't any Martians to shoot anyway; might as well practice on something real."

"And what if I don't?" I said, still yelling. "Maybe he won't even be allowed to go. Maybe he doesn't even have a license." Out of the corner of my eye, I could see Peter shaking his head at me, but I ignored him.

"And maybe he does," Dad barked. "It can't hurt to ask. You don't, I will. What's his number?"

I felt like a balloon whose air had been let out; I knew he'd call. And I knew he'd get his way like he always did. "Okay, okay, I'll ask."

Dad put his cup down. "No," he said quietly. "No, *I'll* ask. For all I know, you'll just *say* you asked, say his folks said no. This way, I'll be sure. Grayson," he said, like he was switching tactics, "you're a damn good shot, son. Hunting's a good sport for you. You hunt, you'll always have friends; you'll be respected. It's time you used that training I got for you back in Massachusetts. Hey, at your age, Pete'd already gotten his first deer!"

"Dad, leave it," Peter said softly. "Everyone doesn't have to like hunting."

I looked at Mom again, but she picked up her coffee cup and hid behind it. "I'm not Pete," I said. It came out a lot softer than I'd meant it to, sort of like a bleat, but Dad heard it anyway.

"No," Dad said, "you're not. And you don't have to be. But it wouldn't hurt for you to be a little more like him. You do have to grow up to be a man in a man's world. What's Ross's number?"

So Dad called and Ross's dad said great, and come Saturday there we were, crouching in a bunch of reeds and tall grass by the shore in the freezing cold, even though Mom's "bright October weather" was supposedly going to last till Sunday. Maybe so, but the sun was just beginning to come up and nobody had told it to come up hot. Ross and I, with Barker between us, were shivering at one end of a sort of inlet, staring out at the water through binoculars. Ross didn't have a license, but he'd jumped at the chance to go. And now I could tell Dad really liked him in spite of his computer games—liked him better than me it had looked like when Dad was showing him how to hold Peter's shotgun.

"Sure beats staring at little purple people on a computer screen, doesn't it, son?" Dad whispered to Ross.

That kind of irked me, Dad calling Ross "son."

"Sure does, Mr. Wilton," Ross said enthusiastically.

I wanted to throw something, maybe even at someone, but I felt Barker tense, and Peter, who'd been quacking with the duck call, suddenly pointed out over the water. "There's a nice pair," he whispered.

"You take 'em, Pete," Dad whispered back. "Show the kids how."

We all watched Peter-the-Great-White-Duck-Hunter lift his gun and squint at the two ducks. I had to admit he looked pretty damn professional when he aimed and fired. There was a splash, a squawk, and a flurry of wings; one bird rose smoothly, the other jerkily, then fell. "Get it, Barker," Pete ordered, but Barker had already bolted out of the underbrush. I hated to see Barker do that! Why did he have to love hunting innocent birds so much?

When Peter and Barker came back with the duck, I saw Ross look at Peter like he was some kind of god.

"Whoa-ho, Peter!" Dad thumped Peter-Duck-Hunter on the back. "Was that a shot or was that a shot? You're damn good, son, damn good. See that, kids?" he said to me and Ross. "That's how it's done. Now, Ross . . ."

◇ ◇ ◇

By the time we got home, we had six ducks. Three were Peter's, two were Dad's, and one was mine or Ross's. No one was sure which because we'd both fired at just about the same time, me with Dad's gun and Ross with Pete's. Of course it was illegal for Ross to shoot, but Dad said it was just for practice, and after all, he himself was an experienced hunter, so it was perfectly safe. I guess he figured the law wasn't written for him.

Like I said, we couldn't tell whether it was me or Ross who got the sixth duck, but Dad gave it to Ross anyway. Figures, right? Not that I really wanted it; it was the way he did it, like it couldn't possibly have been me who'd shot it, even though I was about as good with a gun as I was with a bow. Maybe I was mad at Ross, too; Jemmy'd probably have said I'd shot it and we'd have fought over which one of us should have it, like in the Alphonse and Gaston joke Mom told us once when Jemmy and I each tried to let the other go first like the two French guys in the joke. It really cracked us up, so we used to do it a lot.

Anyway, Ross was the guest, so I guess it was, you know, polite to let it be his duck, and like I said, I sure didn't want the duck, which looked damn miserable, dead. But it was like as far as Dad was concerned, I wasn't really there, even though he'd made such a fuss about me going in the first place. And I guess it sort of made me think maybe Ross and I weren't going to be as good friends as me and Jemmy.

"Pretty damn good," Dad said gleefully when we dropped Ross and his duck off and headed home. "What a morning, eh, boys?"

"Great morning, Dad," Peter said. "Thank you."

"How about you, Gray?" Dad said, like he'd just noticed me. "Better than shooting Martians, right?"

"Yeah, sure," I told him.

But it wasn't. The aliens we shot at weren't beautiful and free. And the ducks hadn't ever hurt anyone in their whole lives.

I was going to write Jemmy about the duck hunt, or call him, but at lunchtime that day, Mom brought up the subject of my drums again and Dad finally promised he'd talk to the neighbors about me practicing at full volume. The drums at school were okay, and Mr. Halifax let me work on them after school sometimes, but they weren't as good as my drums, and that loose head on the bass still hadn't been replaced. But Dad must've felt guilty or like he owed me a favor since I'd gone hunting, because after lunch he started calling the neighbors, and then he went out to see the people on the other side of us from the Mallers. I hung out in the kitchen pretending to do homework for at least an hour while Dad was out. It was almost four o'clock when he came back, and Peter, who'd taken a duck over to the Mallers' at around lunchtime, was still over there. Man, I was so nervous my mouth was dry, like I was thirsty even though I wasn't.

"Okay," Dad announced when he came in. "It's all set. The neighbors agree. One hour from four to five on Saturdays, and only in the basement. The rest of the time you can practice at school or with those silencer things."

I bolted for the basement before I could forget the new song that had come into my head overnight; I'd pretty much finished the other one at school and I really wanted to work on the new one before I tested the older one. But Dad grabbed my shoulder as I passed. "How about 'Thanks, Dad'?"

"Yeah, sorry," I said. "Thanks, Dad." I tried on a smile. I guess I was grateful, but one hour a week at full volume wasn't a whole lot, and I didn't want to waste any of it. "Really. Thanks!"

Dad squeezed my shoulder for maybe only the third time since Suspension Number Two, then let it go. "You're welcome," he said. "At least that's something that you're good at and that you like, which I know isn't true of hunting. So go down there and beat the hell out of those drums. Just remember, only one hour. And"—his voice followed me down the cellar stairs—"when you're rich and famous, don't forget it was your old man who made it possible."

How in heck, I thought as I nearly tripped over Mom's laundry basket in the unfinished part of the cellar, *can he think he's making it possible by only letting me have one hour a week on my own drums without practice pads? And as far as liking stuff I'm good at, what about archery? At least he doesn't make me kill animals with my bow!*

I got really mad, thinking that. Then I banged my shoulder on a corner of Dad's gun cabinet, which was just inside the door to the finished section of the cellar, right next to the small blocked-off place that was my practice room. I ducked into my practice room in such a hurry that I knocked against the cymbals as I slid onto the drum throne, thinking, *Why doesn't he like anything I'm good at?*

I ripped off the tarp I kept over my drums, kind

of as if it was part of Dad or maybe part of the Bruce and Hank clones at school, who by the way were getting harder to ignore, and I tuned each drum, picked up some sticks, flexed my wrists, did a practice roll, and then stamped on the pedal, hammering the bass.

Not right yet—and five minutes wasted. I tightened the bass head more and tried again.

Better. Much better. Okay.

I closed my eyes and got to work. The melody had come easily and I'd strummed it quietly on my guitar at 3:00 A.M. before we went hunting, and then added some chords. But it needed more, a foundation, something to anchor it. . . .

In about half an hour, I had it. God, it felt good! And I felt good, better than I'd felt since we'd moved. So I leaned back and just jammed, letting my hands zip from drum to drum, my foot rock on the pedal, and my body move to the beat. The music filled me, chasing everything else away, especially the bad stuff going on at school, as the music always did when it was loud and right. This was happiness, this was joy, this was the only thing worth anything, this was who I was. . . .

Suddenly the lights flicked off, and Dad's voice bellowed down the stairs. "Gray! How many times do I have to tell you? Time's up!"

Okay, so I heard him, but it was as if he was far away, so far away maybe I *hadn't* heard; the voice was on the moon maybe, or maybe I was, and it takes a long time to pull a guy back from the moon, so I kept playing. *I am the music now, the beat is my heart, my lungs, my soul . . .*

"Gray! Goddamnit, cut it out! If you can't keep your end of the bargain, you're not going to be able to practice here at all! Come on, quit, before the neighbors start calling."

The words just rolled over me at first. But then I heard this thump and I felt him grab the back of my neck. He yanked me off the throne and shook me till my head snapped back. It hurt so much that the music left me and I could see his bloated, red, ugly, angry face.

"Dad, damnit, stop, you're hurting me!" I tried to smash his ugly face, but he was shaking me too hard; I couldn't get my arms to work.

"I'll hurt you even more if you go overtime again! You're a real genius at defiance, aren't you, boy? What the hell does it take to teach you? God knows I keep trying, but nothing takes. Give you an inch and you take a mile! Well, this is the last mile you're going to take for a while! We're new in this neighborhood, and I'll be damned if you're going to spoil things for us again!"

Partway through his yelling I gave up trying to hit him. Instead I closed my eyes and tried to make my body go limp. I knew from a couple of other tantrums he'd had since Suspension Number Two that it hurt less that way. Besides, I wanted to hold on to my song, but Dad was shaking me to a different beat, and that one took over.

"Harry, for God's sake! What are you doing? Harry, stop!"

I heard Mom running down the stairs, and suddenly I realized Dad had stopped shaking me; he let me go. As I fell back against the drums, clattering them, I saw his red face again. His eyes looked sort of like there were tears in them, but I'm pretty sure it must have been sweat.

Then Mom was there, kneeling, her arms around me. "Are you all right, honey? Dad just lost his temper, he . . ."

But I couldn't take that. I pushed her away, picked myself up, ran up the cellar stairs and out of the house.

◇ ◇ ◇

I kept running past all the ticky-tack houses and along all the curvy streets, only I wasn't looking at any of them or anything. I wanted to get so winded I couldn't think, but after a while my neck and my head hurt so much I had to stop. So I just sort of sat down where I was, and after a while my face felt wet and when I licked it, it tasted salty. So I got hold of myself and looked around to see where I was. I kind of hoped I was nowhere, you know? In some nowhere place where nothing could ever happen.

But I was in a vacant lot, sitting on a scratchy old cement block with weeds growing through it and tall grass all around, and I could see that it was getting dark.

I remember thinking that maybe I was lost, and I thought of that dumb college song Dad used to sing about little lost sheep—lambs, I think; poor little lambs—it goes *"baa, baa, baa"* in the chorus. I think I sort of went *"baa, baa, baa"* myself, and then I got up and went out of the lot to find a street sign, but I wished like hell I was still in Massachusetts and could go see Jemmy.

Mom met me at the door when I finally got home. It was like she must have been right at a window. Her face was sort of gray-looking and her eyes were scared and sad under her frizzled hair. I thought she was going to yell, but she just put her arms around me and held on tight.

Then Dad thumped into the hall and yelled, "Where the hell have you been? Your mother's been worried sick."

I think I might have said, "And you haven't, right?" I know I thought it.

He took a couple of steps like he was going for me again, but Mom somehow found the guts to get between us. She said, "Leave it, Harry," and he stopped and I ran up to my room fast and slammed the door.

And I remember thinking that between Zorro and Johnson and Dad and drums, "gonna change" was doing a damn good job of turning into "gonna get worse." By then I didn't even feel like talking to Jemmy anymore, or to anyone.

FALCO: Had your dad ever hit you before, Gray? Like when you were little? Had he hit Peter?

GRAY: Never Peter. Not me, either, when I was little. But yeah, like I said, a couple of times since Suspension Number Two.

FALCO: Mmm. It's almost like he didn't know what to do with you. Like he didn't trust you after what happened at Parker. What do you think?

GRAY: Right. He sure didn't trust me! He trusted Peter okay, but not me. Not since the stuff at Parker. I think he was embarrassed that one of his supposedly perfect sons got suspended. Sons he wished were perfect, anyway.

FALCO: Were you jealous of Peter?

GRAY: Jealous? I don't know. Was I? I'll have to
think about that.

FALCO: Please do . . . Wait a sec, I have to put a new
tape in . . . There. Okay, let's see now. Peter,
right? Peter had pretty good luck with girls,
didn't he? Lindsay next door . . .

GRAY: Yeah, he did. I don't know. Maybe I was
jealous. I liked Peter; some, anyway. Most of
the time. Lately, though, I don't know. Since
he started high school he was, I don't know,
sometimes playing big brother too much,
maybe, like I was still about six years old. And
girls, Lindsay—well, there was this really bad
day—good, too, in a way, but bad, too. A bad
good day, maybe. Peter was sick . . .

It was early morning. Rain. Dark sky. Water sliding
down the windows. I tried to remember the game
Mom used to make us play. Name the raindrops,
then race them. This one's Jim, that one's John, see
which one'll get to the bottom first.

Peter's always was John, and his almost always
won.

I shoved my math book and my social studies
book into my pack. Then I saw my boring unfinished
homework—gotta work on that, I knew—and stuffed
that in. What else? My knife was already inside my

sock, hiding from searches, especially the one Dad had been putting me through a couple of mornings a week ever since I'd gone AWOL after that bad drum-practice day, because, he said, he couldn't trust me anymore. I didn't get the connection, but I guess he thought there was one. He'd have taken my knife away by now if he'd spotted it, so I knew he didn't really know I was carrying it. I'd done a little sort of general complaining about the varsity guys, feeling my way with him about it; maybe that had made him suspicious. It sure would've been nice to really talk to him about Zorro and company, but the couple of times I'd hinted, he'd just said stuff like "Keep your shirt on. Don't let them see you react," and "Remember, we don't want any repeats of what happened at Parker."

Big help, right?

Anyway, The Searches. He always searched me on a different morning, not every Monday or every Wednesday or whatever, like that was going to fool me, catch me off guard. If Dad had really known what was going on at school with the varsity guys, I bet he wouldn't have bothered; he might even have wanted me to take a weapon. Would he have? No, I guess not. He'd just have said I should use my fists if anyone started a fight with me. Well, yeah. Nothing

I'd have liked better, Dad. It'd sure have beaten banging said fists against the walls of my room, which
I'd been doing a lot lately. I wondered if he really
thought I could fight off the whole varsity football
team, or even only a couple of them, with just my
fists. Not even Perfect Peter could have done that.

Of course he'd never have to, that was for sure.

Pretty soon I heard Dad yell, "Gray! Get a move
on! You'll miss the bus, damnit! And I've got to
leave."

"Yeah, Dad, okay."

So, I thought, slipping my pack over my shoulder and saying *"Fuck you!"* under my breath as I went
downstairs, *today's a search day. Wonder if he knows how
transparent he is?*

"Where's Pete?" I asked, making distracting conversation when I got to the kitchen and handed Dad
my pack. Pete hadn't been at breakfast and I hadn't
heard him leave.

"Sore throat," Mom said, looking up from maybe
her third cup of coffee. "And temperature."

"Lucky stiff."

I held out my hand for the pack when Dad had
finished searching it, and I rubbed one ankle casually
against the other, feeling the knife, grinning inside.

"Good boy," Dad said absently, nodding.

As if I were a dog, I thought, charging out of the house into the rain. Sit, stay, come, lie down. Behave.

◇ ◇ ◇

Lindsay was already at the bus stop, her yellow slicker bright against the dark morning, her lips glowing pink against her white skin, and her long pale hair hidden under the slicker's hood. I liked her hair; it looked soft, smooth. I'd never touched a girl's hair. *Maybe I'll touch hers one day,* I thought.

Or Daisy's.

"Hi, Gray." Lindsay smiled, then looked expectantly toward the house.

Of course, I thought grimly. Yeah, I guess I was jealous then, and still mad at Dad about The Search, too.

"Where's Peter this morning?"

"Languishing in bed," I answered. "He's got a sore throat. Mom thinks it's terminal."

For a moment Lindsay looked startled. Then she laughed. "Poor Peter," she said. "Does it hurt really bad?"

How should I know, I thought. *I'm not his goddamn throat!* "I don't know," I said out loud. "I haven't seen him this morning."

Lindsay looked embarrassed, sorry. "You guys seem so close, I just thought . . ."

I shrugged. "I guess we're close in some ways," I said begrudgingly. *Are we?* I wondered. We used to be, before Pete started treating me like a little kid. And since The Suspensions, it was like Dad saw us as a sort of variation on good cop/bad cop—good son/bad son. I wasn't sure Mom agreed, but like I said, she usually didn't go against Dad unless things got really bad. Anyway, Pete and I didn't connect much anymore. It was great when we did, like that time when we didn't look too hard for our good clothes when we were going out to dinner our first night in Greenford. But stuff like that was happening less and less. It was different now, like everything else.

Lindsay and I both stood there in the rain, looking down the street where there was no sign of the bus. Then I heard tires screech, and we both wheeled around as Dad's car shot out of the driveway, skidded as it turned, and careened away.

"Your dad must be late," Lindsay said. "He doesn't usually drive like that."

"No." I knew if Dad really was late, it was me he was mad at for taking my time getting ready for The Search. "He doesn't." I shifted my pack, which was getting wet. So was I; the water was rolling under it and soaking through the back of my jacket.

"So," said Lindsay, "how are you liking high school?" Then she said, "Wow," quickly, as if she'd just noticed that I was staring at her. "That's a dumb question! I must sound like an aged aunt or something. Sorry."

I think I sort of smiled at that. "Yeah," I said. "A little dumb. High school's okay. Some of it, anyway. Everything but the classes. Three o'clock's good, too."

She laughed. I liked the sound, like she was really happy I'd been so wonderfully funny.

"I've seen you with Ross Terrel, having what looked like a good time."

"Yeah? Where?" I felt sort of spied on till I realized, no, she wouldn't spy.

"In the library. At the computers."

"Oh, yeah."

"You like computers?" she asked as the bus finally rounded the corner and headed toward us.

"They're okay. Distracting, you know?"

She nodded. "Are you guys online?"

Saved by the bus! It pulled over in front of us before I had to answer. "Well, see you," I said, not answering Lindsay's question. It was embarrassing to have to tell people I wasn't allowed to use our computer, and this morning it was making me mad to think about it. I hurried onto the bus ahead of her because I knew she'd want to sit with her friend, that Hannah kid, who looked and acted like a puppy.

Weird combo, but then I figured maybe people might think me and Ross were weird together, too. I wondered if people had ever thought that about me and Jemmy.

"Have a nice day," Lindsay called after me.

Yeah, right, I thought, still in a crummy mood and already steeling myself for the usual morning jock assault. I'd been thinking about that half the night, too. Ross had told me his dad had joined the "just-ignore-them" club the other day when Ross had tried to talk to him about it. Sure. We were still trying, but that was getting a lot harder to do.

⬡ ⬡ ⬡

"Hey, lookee here! It's Crater Face and Nerd Brain Camo Girl!"

Ross rolled his eyes and elbowed his way past the varsity jocks, who despite the rain were clustered on the steps again instead of near the lockers, which is where they usually hung out. I touched one ankle to the other, feeling the knife, wondering if this was when I was going to have to pull it out, and trying to tell myself, *Yeah, you can do it.* But I ran up the steps, too. "Too dumb to come in out of the rain," I muttered, head down to keep it from being punched as I passed the jocks and their friends.

Correction. *Tried* to pass. Someone grabbed me

from behind this time, and I felt a weird sort of scared squinch in my throat that made me think about the knife again. The other guys closed in around me, circling quickly, cutting me off from Ross.

"What did you say?" asked Zorro, who I realized was the one who'd nabbed me. I never had caught his real name. Devon? Eugene? Edmund? Some fancy name like that, a name I guess might once have gotten him the treatment he gave me. But "Zorro" never seemed right for him; I mean, wasn't Zorro some kind of folk hero or something? This guy didn't seem to like very many folk outside of the guys who always followed him around.

"You heard me," I snarled through the sudden coppery fear-taste in my mouth. That made me madder still.

"No, Crater Face, I missed it. Hard of hearing, you know?" Smirking, the folk hero slapped my ear. It made a quick roaring sound, like a seashell. Then it hurt, and I started snaking my hand down, reaching for the knife—thinking about pulling it out, anyway.

But Mr. Gomez, the Spanish teacher, ran up the steps and into the circle, saying, "Break it up, fellas, break it up. Bell's going to ring. Come on, kid." He put his arm over my shoulder, hurrying me inside.

I guess I was sort of glad his arm was there, but I

wondered if he heard one of the jocks say, "Awwwrr, wook at widdle wuss-face" as we passed.

By that time I knew GHS had all kinds of fancy policies against fighting and stuff, but I also knew no one, meaning teachers and administrators, liked to apply them to jocks. I also knew that guys at GHS on varsity teams like football didn't have to go by the same rules as the rest of us and that they had special privileges, even days off around the time of big games.

All morning I wanted to kill Zorro so much it scared me, and I decided it was time to try to fight at least one of those guys first chance I got. Suspension or no suspension.

All afternoon I planned how I could get one of them alone, preferably Zorro. Just me; I didn't even tell Ross. I didn't know why that time on the steps was any different from the others, but sometimes you've just had enough and it all boils over. Must have been that temper I'm supposed to have and the bad mood I was in to start with.

Anyway, what really clinched it was a little later when Zorro and Johnson went through their usual routine with us in the locker room, only this time they got rougher, and when they pushed they pushed super hard, and Ross got his head banged real bad on his locker just before Mr. Vee came in. Then Johnson and Zorro were all nice and polite and like, "Yes, sir, we're just about to change. Just waiting for the kids to get through, just giving them some space, you know."

Mr. Vee looked as if maybe he hadn't fallen for it, but I could tell he wasn't about to interfere. All he said was, "Well, okay, boys, hurry up. It gets dark early, you know, these days."

So I was still stewing about that after school, and I told Ross I was going to hang around for a while. The rain had finally stopped, and after Ross went home, I waited outside till football practice was over and the varsity guys were dressed and leaving. I still wasn't really sure if I was going to do anything or not, but when I saw that Zorro wasn't with the others when they left, and there was no sign of Johnson, I went on waiting.

Finally Zorro came out of the main building with a pile of books but without Johnson; I decided maybe he'd had a late tutoring session or something. Anyway, I went up to him.

"Hey, Crater Face," he said. "Whassup?" He almost sounded friendly, but I knew it was fake.

The words just came out. I didn't even think about them. "What's up is that my name's Gray Wilton, not Crater Face, and Ross's name is Ross Terrel, not Camouflage Girl or Nerd Brain, and we're both pretty sick of you and your sidekicks beating on us." And I swung at him.

I would've connected, too, if his pal Johnson hadn't shown up just then and grabbed me before my fist connected with Zorro's ugly face.

"Jeez, Crater Face," Zorro said, grinning, "you really ought to take some boxing lessons or something."

"Yeah," Johnson said. "You show him, Z."

Johnson was still holding me, and I was squirming around some, but he was pretty strong and I couldn't get loose.

Zorro stepped back and eyed me up and down. Then he squinted and held up his hand like a painter measuring perspective or whatever it is painters are doing when they do that, and then he let fly with his fist and it jabbed me right in the eye.

Johnson gave my arm a twist. Then he let me go and I kind of fell down, grabbing my eye, which hurt like hell.

Johnson gave me a little shove with his foot, and he said very softly, "Don't try to lecture your betters, fag," and he and Zorro walked away laughing.

For a minute or two I thought I couldn't see out of either of my eyes, but then I realized the ground was muddy from all the rain, and I had mud mixed with, okay, I guess a few tears and maybe blood in both eyes. I sort of rubbed at my face with my hands and staggered over to one of the benches at the far end of the parking lot, where I tried to calm down and put myself together. My jacket was torn and the arm Johnson had twisted hurt, and so did its shoulder. Then as I started rubbing it, who should come by but Lindsay and Hannah.

I really should work on that invisibility, I thought.

Lindsay put her hand on Hannah's arm, stopping her. Then she whispered something to her. Hannah left, and Lindsay came over to me.

"Gray? Are you okay?" she asked. She put her hand out as if she was going to touch me, but I guess I didn't look too eager for that, because she pulled it away again. It's funny, though. I almost wanted her to, you know, touch me. Then she sat down next to me and said, "Sorry. That's another dumb question— two in one day. You're not okay. 'What happened?' would have been a better one. What happened?"

I shrugged, I guess, which made my shoulder hurt worse. I sort of wanted to tell her because I wanted to tell someone, but right then I wanted to tell someone who could make it all stop and I knew she couldn't, so I just said, "Fell in the mud."

"Must've been quite a fall," she said, and I could see she didn't believe me. "Here." She took a tissue out of her pocket and brushed my face with it, like

Mom might've. Then she pulled away and said, "Maybe you'd better go in and wash. Your mother'll freak if she sees you like this."

"No," I said. "No, I . . ." But I couldn't think what to say next, so I said no again. Part of me wished she'd go away and another part wished she'd stay forever.

"How about we get on the late bus when it comes," she said, "and go to my house? That way you can clean up before you go home."

I nodded. I mean, it did sound like a good idea. I knew I had to clean up before Mom saw me, and I sure didn't want to go back inside school. I hadn't seen Zorro and Johnson actually leave the school grounds.

So we waited for the bus and didn't say anything anymore. I kept feeling like what I really wanted to do was go to sleep, and then maybe go down to the cellar and do some practicing without the practice pads. I think I was almost asleep when Lindsay said, real quiet, "Who was it, Gray?"

I was kind of startled at that because it meant she'd figured out I'd been lying about falling in the mud, but I guess she'd have had to be pretty dumb to believe that, and Lindsay Maller sure wasn't dumb. But I knew I couldn't tell her or anyone, so I just shook my head.

"Okay," she said, sort of sighing. "I won't pry. But if someone's giving you a hard time, you should report it to the principal or the student government and they'll . . . ."

"No!" I said, loud, so she'd know I meant it and would stop with that idea. "No. That's not how it works."

"How what works?"

Hell, I thought, *if she's figured out as much as she seems to have, she ought to be able to figure that out, too.* But I wasn't about to explain it to her.

"How what works, Gray?"

I looked away from her, watching for the bus and for green Fords.

◯ ◯ ◯

When we got off the bus, Lindsay sort of turned me toward her house, but I said, "It's okay. My mom won't be home. She's at work. I'll just go on in."

"You sure?"

"Yeah, thanks. I'm sure."

She gave me a look like she was trying to see through me or something, and then she said, "Well, how about I come in with you and say hello to Peter, see if he wants me to bring his homework if he's going to be absent again tomorrow?"

Peter again, I thought. *Maybe he's what this is really about. As usual. She's too old for me anyway, right?*

"You can if you want to," I told her. Then I realized she'd better not mention what I looked like, because then my whole family would freak and yell. I started to ask her not to, but I couldn't think exactly how. "Only . . ." was as far as I got.

"Only what?"

"Only just . . ." I looked at her, hoping she could figure it out.

"Only don't tell Peter what happened to you?"

"Yeah," I told her. "I mean, I'll say something to him, maybe, but . . ."

"But you'd rather do it in your own time."

"Yeah." *When I figure out what to say,* I told myself. I really didn't want Pete to know I'd gotten creamed.

Or anyone.

"Okay."

So we went on into my house, and I stopped at the stairs and yelled, "Pete? Company! You decent?"

What the heck, I thought. I knew if I was sick and it was Daisy downstairs, I'd sure want her to come up!

Remember Daisy? When the weather started to get colder, instead of blouses with the skirts she always wore, she started wearing soft, fuzzy sweaters that sometimes showed the small mounds of her breasts and the smaller outlines of her nipples. She started putting pale shiny stuff on her lips, too. I don't remember what it's called. I'd been smiling at her for weeks, and she'd been smiling back; she had the warmest, friendliest smile of anyone at Greenford High. Finally I'd said hi to her and she'd said hi back, and I'd made a point of saying it every day from then on so I could hear her answer. She'd even said, "How're you doing?" a couple of times.

That was one good thing.

Anyway, when I called up the stairs to Pete, there was no answer, so I called again.

Still nothing.

"Maybe he's sleeping," Lindsay said.

I gave her a smile. "You could wake him up, then. He'd like that, I bet. Come on."

I led her up the stairs and showed her where Pete's room was, and then I went back down again and headed to the bathroom to clean up. Then I realized I'd better get a washcloth, so I went back upstairs and got a clean one from the linen closet. I could hear soft voices coming from Pete's room and I wanted to look in but I figured they'd see me and Pete would be mad, so I went back down and tried to wash the mud off. It really hurt, especially around my right eye and on my right cheek. I couldn't tell where the mud stopped and the bruises began. My arm hurt, too, and my shoulder, but I couldn't see any bruises there.

I took the muddy washcloth down to the cellar and put it in Mom's laundry basket. When I went back upstairs, Lindsay was in the kitchen.

"Peter wants juice," she said.

"Fridge," I said, pointing. "How do I look?"

"Not great." Lindsay opened the fridge, took out a carton of OJ, got a glass out of the cupboard, and poured. Then she came closer to me and peered at my face. "I think you're getting a black eye. And a black cheek. I don't think you're going to be able to hide them."

"Yeah, that's what I thought," I said. "Listen . . ."

"I won't say anything," she said quickly. "I don't know what happened anyway, and that's what I'll say if anyone asks. You say whatever you want."

"Thanks." I got myself a glass and had some juice myself. It felt nice and cool going down.

Lindsay opened the freezer compartment and handed me an ice tray. "Try putting some ice on your eye."

"I thought it was steak you're supposed to use. Maybe rib eye," I said, trying to be funny.

She didn't laugh, so I guess it was another one of my falling-flat jokes. "I don't know if that really works," she said. "But go ahead if you have any."

I looked in the other part of the fridge, but I didn't see steak, so I took the ice tray to the sink. "Guess not," I said, popping cubes.

Lindsay took a dish towel off the rack, wrapped some ice in it, whacked it a couple of times against the counter, I guess trying to smash the cubes, and put one hand behind my head. With the other, she held the towel against my eye. She was really gentle. *Lucky Pete,* I thought. So okay, maybe I was jealous then, too.

"Hold this," she said. "Don't leave it on too long. You don't want a frozen eyeball."

I laughed. *Her* joke deserved it, at least. "Thanks again," I told her.

"You're welcome. Gray, listen." She picked up Peter's juice. "You really should report it if someone's bothering you."

"Hey," I said, trying to shrug it off, "I can handle it."

"Umm." Again, she sounded as if she didn't believe me. "Okay. But think about it anyway," she said over her shoulder as she left.

I kept the ice on my eye for a couple of minutes, but it got too cold, so pretty soon I went down to the cellar. I sat there in front of my drums, holding the sticks, trying not to feel the ache in my eye and in my arm and shoulder—mad at myself, too, for not being able to get back at Zorro. But even so, it did feel good to have tried. At least I'd shown him I wasn't a total wuss. And, hey, instead of Zorro alone it was Zorro and Johnson—two against one. Yeah, but I must've seemed like a wuss anyway since I'd, like, lost.

Yeah, but two big guys against one skinny guy . . .

I argued with myself like that for a while, and thought about what those guys might pull next, and tried to decide how I was going to explain my eye to Mom and Dad.

Then I wondered what the hell Lindsay was doing up there so long with Peter. I mean, he *was* sick! I didn't think they could possibly, you know, be doing anything. Besides, I didn't think Perfect Peter ever had. I was pretty sure he was still a virgin. Not that he'd probably have told me if he wasn't, unless he was, like, bragging, which wasn't a Perfect Peter thing to do.

Finally I heard Lindsay calling me, so I yelled, "Down here," told her how to find the cellar, and greeted her with a drumroll. When I saw her, I pounded the bass, but she wasn't looking at me. She was staring at Dad's gun cabinet.

"My dad's collection," I told her. "It's a pretty good one. He likes to hunt besides collect."

"Oh," she said. "Yes. Peter brought us a duck."

"Yeah, I know. I was there. I shot one, too." I did a louder drumroll, for emphasis.

"Did you?" she said, but she didn't sound as if she cared much.

"Yeah." I could feel myself getting mad again, even though I didn't really want to, not with her. "I just said I did." One more roll, backed with bass this time.

"Should you be doing that?" She nodded toward my drums. "With Peter sick and all? I mean, he does seem pretty sick."

"Yeah," I said, trying not to yell at her. But it was going all wrong. "Yeah, I should be doing it. Pete likes it."

"Maybe not when he has a fever."

Her voice was gentle and kind, but I could tell it was all for Peter, like she'd forgotten about me.

"I'd better go." Her eyes strayed to the gun cabinet again. "I just wanted to let you know I was leaving."

I jumped from the throne, jarring my head a little, and stood in front of the cabinet. "Want to see any of these up close?" I asked her. "I can open it for you; I know where the key is."

"No, no, that's okay. I don't like guns much."

"Girls aren't supposed to, I guess," I said. "My mom doesn't, but she doesn't dare say much." *Shit,* I thought, *that sounds nerdy.* "But some girls do," I went on quickly. "Like guns, I mean. My aunt? She's a pretty good hunter."

"Is she?" Lindsay answered. She seemed nervous, edging toward the stairs.

I edged there, too. "Yeah, she even got a pheasant once. She had it stuffed and everything. You know, not food-stuffing. Taxidermy. It's in her living room."

"Interesting." Lindsay sounded the way adults do when they say "That's nice" to little kids. Then she said, "Look, Gray, I've really got to go." But then she gave me this big smile—and I knew it was all for me, not Pete, so I smiled back.

"Your face doesn't look too bad in this light," she said, still smiling. "Stay in the shadows and you'll be fine. How's it feel, your eye?"

"Okay." It still ached, but I didn't want to tell her that. "You—remember—you won't? . . ."

Before I could finish, she held up her hand, palm out. "Our secret," she said.

Then she said, "Our secret" again, and left.

FALCO: So there you are with a black eye, and your
    parents are going to come home and you're

going to have to tell them something. But what
were you going to tell them?

GRAY: I didn't know for a while . . .

I sat there after Lindsay left and fiddled with the
drums a bit more without thinking about what to tell
them. Instead I thought about Lindsay and that she
was really nice and that Peter sure was lucky because
she obviously liked him. And then my eye started
hurting worse, and I guess that's what reminded me
I'd better figure out what to tell Mom and Dad. I got
an idea but it involved Ross, so I went to the phone
and called him.

After I'd explained to him what had happened
and he'd reacted to it partly like I was this big hero
and partly like he was mad at me for not waiting till
he was there so he could've gone after Zorro with
me, I told him my idea about the black eye, which
was that he and I had been mock-wrestling at his
house and I'd tripped and banged into a chair and hit
my face on it.

"Man," Ross said, "you sure have some
imagination!"

"Yeah," I said, "maybe, but what do you think?
Is that a good story or what? Come on, don't you
think they'll buy it?"

He thought about it for a minute and then he

said, "Yeah, I can't see anything wrong with it. What kind of chair, though?"

"What do you mean what kind of chair?"

"Well, a rocking chair, if it was little, would scoot out of the way, and an easy chair would be too soft, and a—"

"Wooden chair, with a back with pointy things on it that could've gotten my eye."

"Could've put your whole eye out, you mean."

"Well, okay, wooden chair with a hard back."

"Maybe it fell over when you hit it and you got a leg in your eye."

"Why wouldn't that put my whole eye out, too?" It was getting funny and I started laughing. "And maybe my nose and my other eye . . ."

"And they're rolling all over the floor," Ross said, "and I'm trying to pick them up . . ."

"And your cat is chasing them, and . . ."

"I don't have a cat." Ross sounded like he was choking with laughter, and I was, too, and I was thinking maybe he was almost as okay as Jemmy after all, when I heard the front door open.

"Shut up," I whispered. "They're here. Mom anyway; she gets home before Dad. No kind of chair. I didn't notice what kind. Okay? Back me up?"

"Sure." Ross was whispering, like my mom could hear him. "Okay. Good luck."

"Thanks."

We both hung up and I heard my mom call, "Gray? I'm home. Just going to check on Peter. How was your day?"

"Marvelous," I called back because I knew she was already halfway up the stairs.

So I sat down at the kitchen table and tried to look like I was reading my math book, which I'd dumped on the table with my other books after Lindsay and I had come in.

When I heard Mom coming down the stairs I put my hand over my eye like I was leaning my head on it.

"Peter says you brought Lindsay to see him," Mom said, not really looking at me, and going to the fridge. "She's such a nice girl. I'm glad they're friends." She took the juice carton out, filled a glass with OJ, and held it out to me. "Would you take this up to Peter?" she asked. I reached for it, forgetting, and she gave this sort of gasp and, like her mother part was taking over from her nurse part, she said, "Oh my god, Gray! What happened to you?"

"It's nothing." I grabbed the glass, which she'd almost dropped, and put it down on the table. "Ross and I were mock-wrestling and I fell over a chair."

"And hit your *eye*?" She sounded pretty skeptical.

"Yeah."

"How?"

"I don't know, Mom," I said. "I wasn't looking." That struck me as pretty funny, and I laughed, and I guess it struck her funny, too, because this little smile came over her face and she said, "Yeah, I guess not." She took out the ice tray and did the same ice thing Lindsay had done. I wondered if an eye really could freeze, like Lindsay'd suggested. But this time the ice did make it feel better.

Then when Dad came home, I told the same story again and he mostly sort of grunted and said something about not being so clumsy and why didn't I at least go out for wrestling if I liked it so much since I really needed to go out for a sport, *blah, blah, blah*. He did look at my eye pretty hard, though, like he wanted to make sure it wasn't, I don't know, broken or anything.

Or maybe to make sure I wasn't lying about it.

FALCO: How about in school? How did people react?

GRAY: Hey, look, it was just a black eye! No big deal, you know? People get them all the time. This is getting old, you know? Can't we talk about something else?

FALCO: We'll leave it soon. But I need to know what happened when you got to school the next day.

GRAY: Well, let's see. Whoops, not a good line to
    use about a sore eye. Sore eye? There's that
    expression, sight for sore eyes. But this was a
    sore eye looking for sights . . .
FALCO: Gray . . .
GRAY: Okay, okay . . .

In homeroom, Ms. Blanchard—remember, the one
who'd looked scared the first day but wasn't—she
asked about it, and Mr. Wallace asked in math, and
Mr. Halifax asked in music and asked if I wanted to
see the nurse, which struck me as pretty funny because of Mom, you know? And like Dad, Mr. Vee
said maybe I should take up wrestling so I wouldn't
be so clumsy. No one took it very seriously except
Mr. Halifax, who seemed like maybe he wasn't sure
whether to believe the story I was telling about it.
He asked me if there was anything more I wanted
to say, and I said there wasn't, and he said if I ever
wanted to talk to him, I could talk, or I could talk
to Ms. Throckmorton, the guidance counselor.

Oh, yeah, and first thing that morning, like they'd
been waiting for me, Zorro and Johnson rushed me
into the bathroom and before I could even think
about reaching for my knife, Zorro pinned me to the
wall while Johnson guarded the door. Zorro said,
"Quite a shiner you've got, Crater Face."

Johnson laughed and said, "For a minute I thought maybe you'd started shaving; your chin's kind of blue, too."

"So, Crater Face," Zorro said, giving me a little shake, "you tripped over your dog or cat or bird or something and fell against the kitchen counter, right?" He gave my arm a twist, the same arm Johnson had twisted.

"Wrong," I said, trying not to show him that he was really murdering my shoulder. "Ross and I were wrestling and I fell over a chair."

Zorro shook his head. "Bad story. You tripped over your dog. You're good at tripping over stuff, I heard. And you do have a dog, right?"

"Right," I said, only he twisted my arm again, so it sounded more like a squeak, "but I've already told my parents about the wrestling and the chair."

Zorro sighed. "Jeez, I wish you'd stop trying to *think,* Crater Face; you're not very good at it. But okay, just this once. Any more black eyes or anything like that, you get your story from me, you hear?" He gave me another shake and let me go.

"I hear," I said, trying not to rub my shoulder, "but I don't think that's really, um, practical."

Johnson left the door and grabbed me. "How come?" he snarled into my face.

"Because," I said, "I'll probably have to explain

to my parents before you figure out what you want me to say."

Zorro shook his head and put on this weird smile. "You're thinking again, Crater Face. Not a good idea. And you're wrong, because we'll tell you right away. And if for some unexpected reason we don't, you just don't say anything. Got it?"

I was getting pretty tired and, I don't know, pretty discouraged and someone came into the bathroom then anyway, so I just nodded and Zorro and Johnson moved away from me like they didn't even know me.

And two things hit me. One: They were going to try to beat me up again, probably. And two: I was trapped, because there was no way they were ever going to leave me alone, even if I went on being able to sort of sass them like I'd just somehow managed to do.

FALCO: So why didn't you talk to Mr. Halifax? Or to the guidance counselor, that Ms. Throckmorton?

GRAY: Are you kidding? Like I said, I was trapped. I knew if I said anything or did anything like that—hell, I'd already tried!—I'd be dead meat.

Interlude

Juvenile Detention Center

⬡ Thursday, July 18

Hexagons.

His dad's face in one of them, grim, angry, not looking at him, no smile, nothing.

Gray shivered, banged his hand on the hard wall till it hurt.

"Dad does care," Mom had told him, visiting. *"He cares a lot. I caught him looking at old photos of you as a baby and of you and Peter as little boys, and so I got out those old videos and he cried, Gray. He cried while he watched them . . ."*

Gray laughed now and banged his aching hand again, his head once, too.

But Mom's voice went on echoing in his brain.

"This is so hard for him, Gray, so hard. He still doesn't understand what happened to his little boy . . ."

Gray put his hands over his ears, but her voice still echoed, softer now.

"Honey, neither do I . . ."

The door to his cell clanked, shattering faces and voices.

Gray froze. *What now? Who's coming? Dad?*

Yeah, fat chance! He'd only come once.

"Visitor," a guard said, bursting in. "Your lawyer. Some shrink, too, name of Bowen. Come on, kid, move it." The guard took his arm roughly.

Gray wrenched it back. Tried anyway.

Too many people, he thought as the guard tightened his grip. *Too many people messing with me.*

Why can't they just get it over with and do whatever it is they're going to do with me?

The Middle

FALCO: Good morning, Gray. How was your weekend?

GRAY: Oh, cool. I played six games of basketball and
  went to the movies and ate at this really fancy
  restaurant and took a long walk in the woods
  with this really gorgeous girl. How about you?

FALCO: Oh, I flew to Paris with my wife and we
  drove to Switzerland and climbed a few Alps
  and ate in a really fancy restaurant, too.

GRAY: You wish.

FALCO: Yeah. So do you, kid. Listen, I brought you
  something—a newspaper clipping from last May.

GRAY: Yeah? Well, guess what? I don't want to see it.

FALCO: Okay. I'll read it to you, I think you'll be
  interested. "School authorities and other sources
  say the alleged shooter, fourteen, is reputed to
  be an angry loner, addicted to violence in the
  form of shoot-'em-up video games, hunting,
  archery, and the loud, pulsating music he
  often played on his drums. His family told the
  Greenford Times that he had two suspensions

from his former middle school for attempted attacks on classmates. His academic record has been uneven, and most of his recent grades were close to failing." . . .

GRAY: Shit!

FALCO: What do you think?

GRAY: It's a lot of crap, that's what I think! It's like it's about someone else. They don't know anything, man! Can't you see that?

FALCO: Well, it does look to me as if they've got some of it right. It's more the emphasis that's wrong, really.

GRAY: What in hell do you mean, "emphasis"? It's like I'm not a person! Subhuman or something. I *hate* hunting! I didn't play video games that much, not like some kids do! The newspaper people never even heard me play my drums. They should've talked to Mr. Halifax. And what about Barker? What about—what about what those guys did to me?

FALCO: That'll come out. That's why I need you to talk to me, why it was good you talked to my friend Dr. Bowen. That'll help who you really are come out at your trial. I want to get the fairest possible treatment for you, remember. Get you into a better place, maybe . . . Okay, now. I guess

we should get started. Let's see. After the black
eye and the trouble with Zorro and Johnson in
the bathroom, things must've changed for you.

GRAY: Yeah? Maybe. I don't remember.

FALCO: Well, according to your school records, your
marks started dropping, so much they affected
your first-quarter grades. There must've been a
reason for that. Hmm?

GRAY: Maybe. Dunno, really.

FALCO: Hey, come on, Gray! This is for your benefit,
remember? What's with you today?

GRAY: Did you play the tape to that shrink, that
Bowen guy? His questions sounded like he knew
stuff about me.

FALCO: No. He and I just talked. Gray, he wants to
help you, too.

GRAY: Yeah, and it's for my own good, right, *blah,
blah, blah*?

FALCO: It *is* for your own good, Gray. Come on, now.
Last time you said you felt trapped, remember?

GRAY: Yeah. So?

FALCO: So did that affect your schoolwork?

GRAY: I dunno. Maybe . . .

FALCO: Look, Gray, we're getting closer to trial time.
And I still have a lot to learn. If you clam up,
there'll be big gaps in important facts. We want

the judge to treat you fairly, to sentence you
fairly if you're convicted . . .

GRAY: *IF!* Convicted means I did it, right?

FALCO: Yes, right.

GRAY: Well, hell, I did.

FALCO: Right. So . . .

GRAY: Oh, shit. Fuck it! Like I said, trapped! For my
own good? Yeah, right. Nothing's for my own
good, you know? . . . There's nothing I can do,
right, to turn you off?

FALCO: Nope.

GRAY: Man, I wish you'd go away. I wish everyone
would leave me alone, you know.

FALCO: I know, Gray. Son, I know . . . Hey, take it
easy. It'll be okay. We've just got to get through
to the end of the story . . . Easy, now. Easy. We'll
take it slow, okay? . . . Here, blow your nose . . .
That's better. Now, nice and easy. School, your
first-quarter marks. How'd that happen? You
were going to do better, right?

GRAY: Yeah.

FALCO: So what happened?

GRAY: Who knows? I really meant to, you know,
try. Too much bad stuff going on, maybe. I did
try, though. I really tried. But after a while,
sometimes I'd just stare at my books, even math,
and my mind would just kind of go blank, you

know, like it was too tired to think. You're right
about my first-quarter grades. And of course
Dad got on my case then, big time . . .

Stone face, I said to myself while Dad was reading my
first-quarter report. *Don't move, don't show anything,
stone, stone . . .*

Dad looked up. "I thought you were going to
study hard here," he said, like he was squeezing the
words out, he was so mad. "I thought you were
going to do better. But this is the last straw. What the
hell happened?"

"A new place, Harry, new people, new chal-
lenges," Mom said softly.

Dad shook his head. "That's not good enough.
Pete's had to make the same adjustments. His marks
are fine. Great, in fact. His report even calls him a
model student. It's not as if you're stupid, Gray." He
paused, but I didn't say anything. "Look, Grayson,"
he said. "I never believed what you said about that
black eye—that you and Ross were wrestling and
you slipped and hit your head on a chair. Did you
have a fight?" His voice got softer. "Are you having
trouble with someone at school? There's a comment
here about there being a couple of 'teasing incidents.'
What's that about?"

"Nothing," I told him. I sure didn't want to

remind him or Mom of the stuff that happened at Parker. "I don't know what it's about. School's fine."

"Well, then there's no excuse, is there? What happened to your marks?"

It sounded sort of like he was going to answer that himself, so I didn't answer.

I was wrong.

"Answer me!" Dad bellowed.

"Harry . . . ," Mom said. "Look at the music grade." She smiled at me, one of those brave smiles people give when they're trying to make the best of something bad. "That's really wonderful, dear. Not even an A-minus. A full-fledged, perfect A. And your music teacher says 'talented in music.' That's wonderful!"

"Why the hell can't he get As in subjects that matter?" Dad said as if I weren't there. "Music's a frill; music's not going to get him a job or the right friends no matter how much he likes it or how good he is at it!"

That was so not true I had to say something. "It could get me a job," I told him. "You don't know anything about it."

"I know a hell of a lot more than you do, young man," Dad yelled.

"Not about music, you don't," I yelled back.

Barker, lying on the floor between me and Dad,

sat up and whined. Then he scrunched over closer to me and leaned against my legs. I let my hand sit on his head, between his ears. *Chill, Gray,* I tried to tell myself.

Barker twisted around and licked my hand, then turned back, staring anxiously at Dad.

"Gray! Harry! Please!" Mom said. "We won't solve anything by yelling. Gray, honey, your father and I think that what you need is a plan. A study plan." She smiled again, like she was trying to encourage me. Or like she was begging me to agree.

"And that study plan," Dad said, "is going to include dropping band and dropping banging away at those useless drums in the cellar until you learn how to study. I don't care how talented your music teacher says you are, your real classes are more important!"

"No!" The word shot out of me so loudly Barker whined again and leaned harder. I rubbed his chest to try to calm us both down, but then I realized my hand was so tense I probably was rubbing too hard, so I stopped.

Dad looked triumphant, like he'd just murdered a whole brace of ducks. "That got you, didn't it? Got you to notice."

"How about," Mom said anxiously to Dad, like she was afraid he'd bite her head off along with mine, "a compromise? How about he drops band after *next* quarter if his marks don't get better?"

"Humph." Dad snorted. "I don't see there's any reason to delay."

"I do," Mom said softly. "He'll work harder next quarter. Won't you, dear?" She beckoned to me, but I stood still, feeling Barker warm against my legs; at least Barker didn't give a damn about my grades. "You're used to the school now, and you've made at least one good friend, so you'll be able to give your schoolwork a really hard try now."

"If he's even capable of a really hard try anymore," Dad muttered. "All right," he said with obvious reluctance. "I'll humor both of you." His voice got a little calmer. "We've got to lick this thing, son. I know parents always say this, but it's for your own good. Every morning before you leave this house," he went on, wagging his finger at me, "I want to see every scrap of homework you've done."

I stared at him, not believing what I'd just heard. I mean, I'd just about decided maybe, okay, I'd try again for the grades, give it another shot anyway. But that kind of killed it, you know?

Out of the corner of my eye I could see Mom was staring, too.

"Harry, really, don't you think—"

"I told you what I think, Samantha. It says right

here"—he waved my report—"it says right here 'Gray started off well in all his subjects, but lately he has often neglected to complete or hand in homework. Seems to lack motivation,' it says. 'Needs to apply himself. Often inattentive in class . . .'"

"Well, surely now that he knows what that's done to his grades, we can trust him to pay attention and do his homework. Can't we, honey?" Mom reached for my hand and squeezed it.

I was still really pissed, but I knew I was caught. The whole conversation seemed pointless anyway. I knew they wouldn't understand even if I explained.

And what would I explain? About Zorro and company? About how nothing really had changed after all? About how Greenford High wasn't much different from Parker Middle as far as the bad stuff went? Yeah, and also about how it looked like I'd be Number-Two Son forever unless I turned into someone I wasn't?

I knew an explanation wouldn't work with Dad in the mood he was in. Wouldn't work even if he was in a normal mood.

The whole thing suddenly made me tired.

Dad lost it then. "See what I mean?" he shouted. "He can't even give a straight answer. What's gotten into you, Gray? You never used to be like this. Pretty soon I'll start worrying about drugs . . ." His voice trailed off and he gave me a look, like he was almost worried instead of mad. "It's not that, is it? Because if it is . . ."

So then *I* lost it. Again. "No, damnit!" I yelled, and this time I almost did add, *It's these guys at school, these jocks who think they own the world,* and suddenly I really did want to tell him the truth about the damn black eye and about how I'd wanted to get back at one of them at least, preferably Zorro, in November, yeah, just using my fists like he'd always said I should if someone else hit first, but doing that hadn't worked because as soon as I'd gone for Zorro, his buddy'd shown up and—well, it was two against one.

But I knew if I said anything like that to Dad, he'd say I shouldn't have sought Zorro out and attacked him, or he'd even start in again about Bruce and Hank and the knife, even though I hadn't used the knife at Greenford yet, just carried it. So instead I went on yelling. "Why the hell are you always so damn suspicious of me? I'm not some—some stupid jerk or something—"

"You are when you act like this." He grabbed my shoulders and started shaking me.

"Harry, no!" Mom said, and she grabbed his arm. It was almost funny, you know, like that little kids' story where people stick to each other if they touch.

All we needed was Pete to bring up the rear of our cheery family parade.

Dad let go, sort of pushing me away, and Mom looked at me with big sad eyes and said, real soft, "Gray, honey, it's only *homework*. Every high school student in the world has homework. Come on, now, be reasonable, hmm?"

Reasonable, hell, I thought but didn't say. *Trapped,* I thought again, too. It wasn't the homework itself anyway; I knew that much. It was Dad not understanding about the stuff at school, and teachers not caring about it when Ross had tried to tell them, and it was Dad not ever trusting me or realizing that I had to keep the knife with me in case things got really bad.

Hell, who was I kidding? I knew he wouldn't even believe me if things *did* get really bad. . . .

"Gray?" Mom was looking at me anxiously, and I could see that she even had tears in her eyes. "Honey? Come on! It's not all that bad, sweetie, and it's not as if you're not bright. I bet you can zip through most subjects if you just *try*."

"Okay," I said finally, muttering it, not meaning it, trapped. But what could I say with her trying so hard and looking at me like that and still hanging on to Dad's arm like she was trying to keep him from attacking me? "Okay, I'll try."

"That's better," Dad said, nodding—still mad, though. "But remember. Every scrap of homework every morning."

"Along with the weapons check, right?" I said through my teeth, and got out of there fast.

◇ ◇ ◇

"What's the point?" I said later to Barker. He'd followed me upstairs; I was lying on my bed listening to my Third Wheel CD, but even that didn't help much. It was like there was this cloud swirling around me, black and thick, trapping me, spiraling me down, making it hard for me to breathe. I think I panicked for a minute; I grabbed my pillow and socked it like I'd socked the wall with my fist sometimes. I didn't want to feel like I did feel, like I couldn't get out of the trap, like I was surrounded, like I couldn't breathe—like there was something wrong with me, like really, *really* wrong. It was kind of scary. I'd never felt that way before, never.

I socked my pillow a few more times, then threw it at the wall. *As if that's going to help,* I thought.

Barker thumped his tail on the floor.

I patted the mattress and Barker jumped up on the bed and licked my face. That made me feel a little better. A little, but not much. I pulled Barker's ears the way he liked. "There's no point, Barker," I whispered. "No damn point at all. Everything I do is wrong anyway. And the thing I want to do forever and get really good at, he hates." It hit me then that I did, I really *did* want that. Music, drums, composing, they were it for me, they were what I'd probably been born for, why I was here. Just thinking about that, about music, made the black cloud a little thinner. Still there, but thinner, like maybe music was the way out of it for me.

You'd think my own father could've figured that out, me and music, I mean, that it was really important, that it was, like, *me,* and that if I could do it, *really* do it, I'd be okay; I'd be who I was supposed to be. Like Pete was able to be who he was supposed to be because he was on the track he wanted to be on, lots of science and stuff at school so he could be a doctor someday.

But I knew Dad hadn't figured me out, and I knew he probably wouldn't because music wasn't on his list of important things and I wasn't on his list of important people. "I bet he didn't even want another kid," I muttered to Barker. "I bet I was a mistake. Or maybe he took one look at me and said to Mom, 'Let's take it back. Let's put it up for adoption.' Or maybe he said, 'You should've gotten an abortion.'" Yeah, I thought, I bet that was it. But I guess Mom stood up to him for once and didn't let him make her do that. So out I popped, probably screaming my head off, which might have been the smartest thing I've ever done. It must've been nice and warm and dark—

Barker lifted his head up, perked his ears.

"Gray?" I heard Peter calling softly. "Gray, you in there?"

"No," I answered.

Peter came in. "Man, it's dark!"

"Yeah, well, guess what? That's what happens when you don't turn on the lights."

Peter sat on the edge of my bed and stroked Barker absently. "Ross came over, but Dad sent him away."

"Figures."

"What's going on?"

"I got a bunch of Ds, one F, and an A in music."

Peter whistled. "Whoa."

"Yeah. He was pissed."

"Well, hey, you can't really blame him, you know?"

"Sure I can. He thinks music is useless. It doesn't count that it's the thing I'm best at. And he thinks maybe I'm doing drugs."

"Are you?"

"No, damnit! But maybe it's not such a bad idea."

Peter shook his head. "It's a bad idea, trust me,"

he said. "And, look, you're good at other things besides music. You're a hell of an archer. You're a good
shot. You're a good runner. And"—he tousled my
hair like I was about three years old—"you're not a
bad guy, either, when you let yourself stay cool."

I shoved his hand away. "Yeah, well, who am I
supposed to believe? You, who're a mere seventeen,
or Dad, who's an expert on everything, even music
careers, to hear him tell about it?"

"Or Mom," Peter said, "who loves you and wor-
ries about you and believes in you."

I snorted, even though I knew he was probably
right. "She never told me that. Not lately, anyway,
not really. And her opinion doesn't count a whole lot
with Dad."

"But she told me. Just now. And she sent me up
here to see how you're doing."

"Oh. Right." I sat up. "In that case you can just
get the hell out. I thought maybe you came up all on
your own. But I guess not. Go on, scram."

"Hey, wait a sec! I'd have come up anyway. The
air's thick down there with the fight you guys had.
You must—I wanted to see how you were, too."

"Out." I lay down again and turned my back on
Perfect Peter.

I could feel that black cloud pressing me down
again.

FALCO: Sounds like a pretty rough scene all around. Did things calm down?

GRAY: I guess. Mostly, you know, things got kind of silent for a while.

FALCO: How's that black cloud now?

GRAY: Huh?

FALCO: The black cloud. Is it still with you?

GRAY: Yeah. Most of the time, anyway.

FALCO: How does it feel now?

GRAY: I dunno. Kind of like it's pressing on me. Like I want to yell, or, I don't know, maybe cry or something. You know. Weird.

FALCO: Unpleasant, I'd say. Hard to take.

GRAY: Yeah, well, I'm kind of used to it, I guess. Like it's part of me now. Nothing really matters anyway.

FALCO: That's pretty tough, I think. Right? . . . Gray? . . . Hey, son, take it easy! Easy . . . Okay. Change of subject. Wasn't it getting close to the holidays around then? Thanksgiving? Christmas? Fun times, or should be, right?

GRAY: Yeah, right. We used to have a good time. Thanksgiving and Christmas.

FALCO: Tell me about Thanksgiving. In the old days.

GRAY: Okay. Yeah . . .

My grandmother was alive till a couple of years ago. Mom's mom. Grandpa died when I was, like, eight or so. We used to go to their house, and there'd be a bunch of aunts and uncles and cousins there, too, people we didn't see very often. I liked this one cousin—Marty, his name was. He and I used to hide under the table when we were really little and eavesdrop on the grown-ups. We'd pretend we were dogs, too, and Grandma would go along with it and feed us stuff. She was cool.

After Grandma died and before we moved to Greenford, we went to this one aunt's house, and that was okay, except we were all a lot older and it wasn't as much fun. We played touch football while dinner was cooking, and that was okay, too, except I was just about the worst player except for one of the girls, Chrissy. We were kind of close for a while. She used to be teased in school because she was fat.

But when we moved to Greenford, we had Thanksgiving at our house. Just us. Everyone else went back to that same aunt's and they called us on Thanksgiving and we passed the phone around at the table, but it wasn't like they were there, you know? Mom made the usual stuff, but the turkey got dry and Dad complained about it and Mom looked like she was going to cry. Pete and I had helped her cook, sort of, but she did most of it, and she got really tired. No one had any fun. Pete kept looking over at the Mallers' house like he wanted to be there. He'd pretty much hooked up with Lindsay by then, only she had an old boyfriend who was away at college and he came home for Thanksgiving. When Pete found out he was going to come, he seemed pretty worried. So we all had problems that day, I guess.

After dinner Pete and Dad and Mom all went to the Greenford High homecoming football game, but the last thing I wanted to do was see Zorro and Johnson strut their stuff. I would've gone to Ross's, but he'd gone to some relative's place with his parents. So I told Mom and Dad I had to study and there wasn't much they could say against that. And I really did study, too. I did all the homework for Monday, and I read ahead in the English and social studies books, and I fiddled around with some extra-credit math problems. And then I took my guitar down to my practice room and worked with it and with my drums without the practice pads for a while. I figured the neighbors were all at the game anyway, or away somewhere having a happy Thanksgiving, so they wouldn't mind. And they didn't. At least no one complained.

It was a really cool practice. I felt great, and a new song I'd been working on was coming along, except I wished I had someone else there to do the guitar part so I could really tell how it went together. I thought that maybe I could get a cassette recorder— you know, like yours—and then I could record one part and play the other, and maybe record it, too, on top of the other if I was really careful. Like, what's it called, mixing? But I guess I'd need a couple of recorders for that, maybe three. Anyway, the big thing I remember about that practice was that again I thought, *Yeah, this is me, this is my thing.* It was like my drums were part of me, I mean really like an extension of my body, my flesh and my blood. I know that sounds weird, but that's how it was. I never felt that way with the drums at school; I guess they just weren't in good enough shape or something. But I sure felt that way with my own drums, whenever I didn't have to use the damn practice pads.

I stopped practicing just in time, too, when everyone came home all excited because Greenford had won. And later I even got Pete to play my new song's guitar part while I did the drums part, but Dad made me do it with the practice pads, so I really couldn't tell how it sounded.

◯ ◯ ◯

School was a zoo on Monday. You'd've thought the varsity football team had won a war or something and saved us all from certain death from the enemy. Ross and I kept hearing applause every time the team or anyone on it walked into a class, and kids bowed and clapped and gave the jocks high fives and pounded them on their backs in the halls, and Zorro and Johnson got a standing O when they walked—okay, strutted—into the cafeteria at lunchtime. Even the teachers treated them like kings, and the girls fluttered their eyes and sounded like they were having orgasms every time they ran into anyone on the team in the hall—not Lindsay or Daisy so much, but Lindsay's friend Hannah and just about all the other girls went crazy for them. I can only imagine what it was like for the girls who had classes with those guys. I was surprised not to see bodies in the halls from people fainting with joy or admiration or whatever. Even Fitz and Morris were kind of excited, if you could say those two could be excited about anything.

Ross and I were disgusted. I mean, here were these creeps being treated like kings and looked up to by everyone when they were just plain ordinary bullies like, Bruce and Hank, who had to have people always thinking they were great in order to think they were great themselves. At lunch we decided not to pay any attention to them, which made Fitz and Morris move to another table, and the whole day we just ignored the jocks, like we couldn't even see them. But I guess Zorro couldn't stand that, because at dismissal he made a point of bumping into us and into the walls, like he was pretending to be blind or something, and of course all his henchmen laughed. Then Zorro said, "Well, let's teach 'em." And he grabbed me by the shoulders and Johnson grabbed Ross, and they walked us real fast out of the building and into the parking lot. By then Ross was looking pretty pale and I guess I was, too, because my legs felt like rubber when Zorro bent me over the hood of his car, which was parked way off on the far side of the lot. He—well, he put his hands around my throat, and I got that coppery fear-taste in my mouth again. I figured Johnson was doing the same thing to Ross, or something like it, and I wondered if maybe they were actually going to kill us this time.

Man, you know what that's like? Really thinking someone might be going to kill you?

FALCO: Terrifying, I should think.
GRAY: Yeah. Terrifying. I guess I was lucky I got
    mad, too, right?
FALCO: I guess. When did you get mad?
GRAY: Right away, I think. On top of being scared.
    See . . .

"Who's king of this school?" Zorro asked.

"Huh?" I sort of croaked.

I could feel his hands getting tighter and it was getting hard to breathe. And then I heard Ross scream. Zorro lifted his knee up and snarled, "You want the same treatment as your little girlfriend? Answer me, Crater Face. Who's king of this school?"

"Shit," I said, and I was mad then, only what I said sounded more like a squeak because he was still squeezing my throat. "You are, you fucking bastard."

"You better believe it," Zorro said, and when he let me go, I muttered, "Self-appointed king and dictator," but I didn't dare say it loud enough for him to really hear.

"Get off my car, you faggot," Zorro said, and he gave me a shove. I fell to the ground and rolled away. Zorro got into his car and peeled out of the lot, with Johnson close behind him.

Ross was crumpled at the edge of the lot, holding his crotch and crying.

FALCO: Jeez. Was he okay?

GRAY: Yeah, but it took a while. I don't think Johnson kneed him really hard. Hard enough, though. And things got worse from then on. I was still going to try to study, you know, to see if I could at least make one thing go better, the

only one I figured I could control. And I did for
a while. But the stuff with Zorro just got worse,
and that sure didn't help any. Like there was
this time when I damn near used my knife . . .

See, I was heading for the music room a little late for
band practice, so the halls were pretty empty. It was
after school and Ross had gone home, but we'd decided I was going to his house after practice. All of a
sudden I was surrounded by jocks and Zorro was in
the middle of the circle. He grabbed my books and
banged on them, going, "Ba-boom, ba-boom, ba-
boom, boom, boom" and made bump-and-grind
motions with his hips. It made me sick, him making
fun of drums that way, you know?

Then Johnson shoved me into the middle, too,
and said, "Dance, fag, dance," and Zorro danced
around me like, I don't know, some stripper or something, the way he was moving his hips. "Come on,
fag, come on, Crater Face, let's see you do your stuff,"
he kept saying. Then Johnson grabbed my hand and
twirled me around a few times till I got so dizzy I almost fell down. And all the time, Zorro was going
"Ba-boom," and the rest of the guys were laughing
and Johnson was saying, "Dance, fag, dance," in between the laughs.

So then Mr. Halifax popped open the band room

door and yelled, "What in blazes is going on here?"
And when he saw, he laughed.

He actually laughed. He's a music teacher, he told
me he loves percussion, and he actually laughed!

At least he stopped pretty quick and he yelled at
Zorro and company and made them leave, and when
he asked me if I was okay, I said yes, because what
could I say to someone whose first impulse was to
laugh?

FALCO: Maybe at first he thought you were a willing
   participant.

GRAY: Shit, man, how could I have been? Would you
   have been?

FALCO: No, of course not, but . . . okay, you're right.
   So was that when you almost used your knife?

GRAY: Yeah. But I couldn't reach it. Sock's a good
   place to hide a knife, but not the best place for
   getting it out, you know?

FALCO: I guess that's true. So how was practice? Did
   you go to Ross's afterward?

GRAY: Practice sucked. I couldn't concentrate. And
   the damn school drumhead was getting worse.
   But yeah, I went to Ross's after . . .

"He's in his room," Mrs. Terrel said when she answered the door. I must have looked pretty awful be-

cause, even though she was wiping at a big blob of something on her apron as I came in, she looked up and then did like the second half of those comedy double takes, and said, "Gray? What's wrong?" and moved toward me like she was going to hug me or something.

I wanted to tell her, to tell someone—a grown-up, you know, who could do something. But it was embarrassing and I didn't want to, like, snivel—that's Dad's word—about it, so I just said, "Nothing," and pushed past her and went up the stairs to Ross's room. By then I could tell I was almost bawling, so I made a detour into their fancy bathroom, and I guess I stayed there for a long time, because in a while Ross banged on the door and yelled, "Hey, you flush yourself down or are you taking a long crap or what?"

I made a couple of grunting noises and flushed and blew my nose while the flush was happening. Then I threw some cold water on my face, dried it with the towel I decided was probably Ross's because it was smudged, and opened the door.

"Yeah," I said. "Must be those cement burgers we had for lunch."

Ross looked at me funny. "Let me guess," he said. "You had a run-in with Zorro and his pals."

I started to say no, but it was kind of nice that Ross had figured it out, kind of like Jemmy would've.

So when we got to his room, I sat down on one of his computer chairs and told him.

"Jeez," he said. "Those bastards. Okay, look. We've got to do something, tell someone. It's never gonna stop if we just go on taking it."

I knew he was right about doing something. I mean, they still waited for us every morning by the main door or down by the lockers, and lately they'd been hissing, "Faggotsssss," as we passed. Sometimes they followed us till the first bell rang, and they bumped into us on purpose a hundred times a day in the halls and sometimes bashed us into the lockers, pretending they'd tripped or something. And every time they knocked us off balance, they laughed like crazy, like it was the funniest thing in the world.

"It's only a matter of time," Ross said, "before they really attack us. I mean really attack, you know, worse. It gets worse all the time, man. In between the bad stuff, they do little stuff, but there's always bad stuff later. We've got to tell."

But I knew we couldn't do that. "We tell, they'll kill," I said. "It's that simple."

"Oh, come on. Kill? They're not going to do that."

"How do you know? They've come damn close so far." I got up and fiddled with one of his model planes, zooming it around. "Besides, who's gonna listen? Mr. Vee didn't exactly listen on the football field back in September, or later when you tried to talk to him. No one else has, either, and no one's done anything. And like I said, Halifax laughed—even Halifax. The teachers don't care, man. Neither does the principal. And your dad and my dad don't have a clue, no matter what we say to them."

I reminded Ross that a couple of times when teachers had been nearby when someone said, "Faggot," or when someone roughed us up a little, the teachers just put on sort of embarrassed smiles and walked on or looked the other way. And once when I'd finally tried saying something to the principal like Lindsay'd suggested, the principal just said, "Well, try to fit in a little better, Wilton, like your brother." Big help, right?

"Forget both our dads," I said to Ross. "And even though Mr. Gomez sort of broke the jock pack up that one time on the steps, and even though he asked me later if I wanted to talk about it, he sure wasn't anywhere in sight later that day when they beat me up, or after Thanksgiving when they ambushed both of us."

Ross sighed. "Yeah, you're right," he said. "So what do you want to do?"

I made the plane crash, only gently so as not to hurt it, and I smashed my fist into my hand like that was part of the crash. "Kill them," I found myself saying, real soft. "Before they kill us."

Ross stared at me.

"Ambush them," I said, only it was sort of not me saying it, like I hadn't really planned to say it. Like it just came out. Okay, I guess I'd thought about it a little around that time, but like daydreaming, not really thinking we'd do it. I'd tried to picture it, though, and how to do it. Somehow I got all sweaty thinking about it, and I'd try to stop picturing it, but I couldn't. I still wasn't too sure I'd really do it, but it was like I was playing with the idea, testing it, kind of. "Ambush them, like they've ambushed us. Maybe with a knife, maybe something worse. Show them we're not fags, we're not wusses like they say all the time."

I felt weird saying it out loud. Excited, not quite scared. Nervous, maybe. Weird.

Ross was still staring at me. Then he gave this sort of short laugh and said, "Yeah, okay, cool. We'll go get us some ray guns and laser guns like in X-Q Killers and splat their brains all to hell."

I laughed, too. It was like it was a joke now, sort of, and that was easier. "Hey, no," I said. "Not that fast. Make 'em suffer."

"Yeah. Tie them up after school after everyone's left."

"After football practice, tie 'em to the lockers . . ."

"Naked."

"Yeah, good. Naked. And then make them march to the main hall . . ."

"No," Ross said—we were both laughing harder, which felt better than weird and sweaty did—"no, to the front steps, tie them there so everyone gets an ugly surprise in the morning."

Ross held up his hand and I slapped it and we went on with what would happen next till we were both rolling on the floor, we were laughing so hard.

Finally Mrs. Terrel came in carrying her usual tray with cookies and glasses of milk on it—she always gave us milk, like we were around nine, but we both pretty much liked it anyway, so it was okay—and she put the tray down on Ross's desk and grinned and said, "You guys sound like you're having fun. It's good to hear you laugh, both of you."

That made us laugh even harder, but we waited till she'd left.

Ross grabbed a glass and downed the milk in it in one gulp. "Okay," he said, putting the glass down and shoving a cookie into his mouth. "Seriously. Serious time."

By then I had my glass in one hand and a couple of cookies in the other and I made a face, exaggerated serious, and Ross cracked up again, which made me crack up again, too.

"Until," he gasped, "until we get those laser guns or handcuffs and rope or whatever, we still need another plan."

"Yeah, okay," I said, but underneath I was wondering if he'd ever go for a *real* plan and if I would, either. Would Jemmy? I kind of thought he wouldn't. I also kind of thought he might even try to talk me out of it, but I wasn't sure of that. Mostly I just wanted Zorro and company to leave us alone, and I didn't want to talk about a real serious plan anymore.

"Like what kind of other plan?" I asked him.

"Like I don't know. But I'd just as soon keep out of their way till we figure something out."

"Yeah, me, too," I said. "But so far the only way we can really be out of their way is to be invisible, especially when we come to school in the morning and leave after school, and when we're in the locker room after PE, not to mention in the halls between classes, which kind of adds up to almost all the time. And damn, but I still haven't perfected my invisibility potion. Only makes you half invisible . . ."

"Which half?"

"Whichever half it wants. Sometimes top, sometimes bottom, sometimes down the middle—right side or left side. Real skinny."

We started laughing again, kidding around instead of thinking about making any kind of plan, real or not so real.

Finally Ross said, "Look, this won't work for the locker room or the halls between classes, but I've got an idea for coming and going."

He explained it to me and what happened was that he had me meet him that Sunday at school for what he called a "dry run" after lunch—dinner, really, at my house, because we had a big meal on Sundays after church. Mom and Dad were busy reading the paper and Peter was away with Lindsay at that youth group winter-retreat thing they'd talked about at the one meeting I'd gone to. Like I said before, he and Lindsay were both on the committee that planned it or something, and now there he was, spending the whole weekend with her at some inn out in the country. Pretty cool, right?

Saturday there'd been some snow, so between church and dinner I was able to play one of my favorite dog games with Barker for a while: throwing snowballs for him and watching him look surprised when they disappeared, which they usually did even when he caught them. That meant I was in a pretty good mood when I met Ross at school.

"Around here," Ross said, leading me across the deserted school grounds.

We waded through ankle-deep snow to a back corner of GHS, and Ross pointed to a small windowless door. "I don't think they ever lock it," he said. "It goes into the basement, near the kitchen." He pulled at the door, but it didn't budge. "Damn!" He kicked it. "I guess they lock it on weekends. But we can try it Monday anyway. We just have to remember to go around to Vesey Street"—he pointed to the side street behind us—"instead of going to the main entrance. We can just go straight out to Vesey from the bus parking lot instead of around to the front. And all we have to do then is go inside and up the stairs from the basement to the first floor and act like we came in the regular way, only we should time it so the first bell's just about to ring."

I nodded. "Cool," I said, and then we went to Ross's house and zapped aliens and jocks and who-knows-what on his computer for the rest of the afternoon. I think that was the day we started calling Zorro and company "the jock pack." Made them sound a little like baby Cub Scouts, you know?

⬡ ⬡ ⬡

As the bus pulled into the lot the next morning, I hunched my shoulders and then relaxed them, trying to ease the ache there and in the back of my neck. When Ross and I got off, Ross pretended to tie his

boot and then, as the other kids ran into the building, he said, real loud, "Shit! I dropped my pen!" and
we both bent down and scrabbled around like we
were looking for it.

"Okay." Ross straightened up when everyone
from that busload was inside. "Let's go."

We took off running around to the side door. A
lot of the snow had melted, so at least we didn't blaze
a trail to the door. I'd worried about that most of
Sunday night. We broke a slushy path leading to the
door, but we didn't leave any clear prints.

"Wait," Ross whispered when, just as we'd almost gotten there, another bus stopped and kids
began filing out. He made a slush ball and threw it
at me. Missed, too. "Wait'll they're all gone."

My slush ball didn't miss and we moved away
from the door, firing slush at each other in case anyone was looking. When that batch of kids was inside
and Ross whispered, "Now," I bent down quickly
before I ran, to make sure my knife was still in place.

"Hey, you guys!" the bus driver shouted as he
drove off. "Wrong way!" He laughed like he thought
he was Mr. Hilarious.

"Damn!" Ross exploded. "He saw us."

"Of course he saw us." I caught up to him.
"How could he miss us? Doesn't matter, though. He
doesn't count. Does he?"

"Nah." Ross shoved against the basement door. "You're right."

This time the door opened easily. "Yes!" Ross whispered as we slipped inside, not that anyone could have heard him above the clanging of pots and the hissing of steam from the kitchen. He slapped my hand in a high five.

My stomach squinched and I nearly passed out from the smell of hamburger. I hadn't felt much like eating at breakfast and I'd slipped most of my toast to Barker when Mom wasn't looking.

"Home free!" Ross chortled when we reached the stairwell. "The jock pack'll never know how we got in. Maybe we can get upstairs without . . . nope!" He put his hand out, stopping me. At the same moment, I looked up and saw that Zorro was standing halfway up on the first landing, his back to us.

"Damn!" I said under my breath.

Ross turned around, pulling me with him. "There's another flight," he whispered. "I think."

He led me along the dim basement corridor to its far end, where there was a narrower stairwell. "I'm not sure where this one goes," he said, leading me up it.

It didn't go to the main hall, but it seemed to go to the first floor, and at least no one was waiting on the narrow landing halfway up, or at the head of it.

But there was no door at the top of the stairs, no

way out to the first floor where both the main entrance and our homeroom were.

"Must be where they take the bodies out," Ross
joked as the first bell rang. "You know, like in hos-
pitals. Secret passage to the morgue."

I laughed, and we went up another flight, at the
top of which was a wider landing with a door to the
second-floor hall where kids were shoving their way
to their homerooms.

"Made it!" Ross said. "Man, this is way cool! We
do this every morning, they'll never catch on."

"Yeah," I answered. Suddenly I felt really good,
hopeful, like maybe we'd solved at least part of the
jock-pack problem. I thought maybe things really
were going to get better after all, and maybe we
could figure out another kind of plan for the halls
and the locker room without doing anything drastic.

We joined the stream of kids flowing toward the
opposite end of the building, which was where the regular stairs led down to the first floor. "You're a genius,
Ross, you know? Can't wait to see old Zorro's face."

"Ugh," Ross grunted. "I can do without his ugly
face."

"Yeah, but picture the surprise on it when he
knows he's been outsmarted."

Ross grabbed my arm. "Now's your chance,"
he whispered. "Morning, man," he said cheerfully,

hurrying me past Zorro, who was standing with his friends at a water fountain. "How you doin'?"

"Shit, it's the baby fags!" Zorro put his finger over the spigot like he was planning to squirt us, but the pressure wasn't strong enough and the water cascaded over the side of the fountain and onto the floor. "Shit!" Zorro said, and shot his wet hand out toward us, showering us both, but only with a few drops.

"Mmmm!" Ross said. "Thanks, man, cooled me down real good." He pulled me into the stairwell and both of us ran down to homeroom, laughing at the jocks for once.

Both of us felt really good then, really hopeful, and for a while after that day, I started paying attention in class again and doing homework. I was practicing drums and writing songs, too, and getting better at both. I even wrote a few pretty good ones, and on a Saturday when I didn't have to use the damn practice pads, I got Pete to play with me on my guitar while I was on my drums. Pete's not too good of a guitarist, but good enough.

That same weekend, I wrote a few of my songs down, and on Monday I decided to show them to Mr. Halifax. Talk about, what is it, butterflies in your stomach? I must've had eagles in mine when I went to the band room.

"Gray," Mr. Halifax said when I was sort of

standing in the doorway thinking maybe the whole thing was a bad idea and I should go away. "Come on in. What's up?"

"I, um, I wrote down some stuff," I said. "I wondered if maybe you'd look at it. It's probably no good anyway, so if you don't have time . . ."

He came over to me and took the music papers out of my hands. "Don't be so hard on yourself," he said. "Have a seat."

It was a good thing he said that because by then my legs felt like spaghetti instead of legs. I sort of collapsed into a chair and he went back to his desk and spent about nineteen hours reading while the eagles chased each other around in my stomach.

And then he reached for his guitar and motioned me to the school drums. "Let's play these," he said, not saying if what I'd written was good or bad.

At first I couldn't get into it, and he stopped playing the chords and said, "Hey, it's okay. Sorry—your 'stuff' is good, Gray. I just want to hear it for real, not just in my head. Okay?"

"Okay," I said, and the eagles settled down. We played my songs, going right from one to another without stopping, and it was really neat playing with him, especially since he was a whole lot better than Pete.

And after the last one, while I was sitting there

on the drum throne with my heart banging like it was a drum itself, he gave me a long look and then he said, real quiet, "Gray, these are really, really good. You know what? I think you need to take real music lessons, like from a professional, and I think in a year or so, or even sooner, you could get a bunch of guys together and have your own band."

So then while I was still sitting there with my mouth open like there was nothing in my head but musical notes, which was about true, I guess, he got up and put his hand on my shoulder. "Tell you what," he said. "I'm going to work out the Christmas concert so you've got some solo work and some good ensemble stuff and we'll see how that goes. And then maybe when your folks come to it and see how good you are, I can talk to them about lessons from this pro I know. You'd probably be able to get a band of your own together from some of this guy's students; there's no one here at GHS who's anywhere near as good as you."

I didn't know what to say, but I finally managed to sort of sputter something lame like, "Thank you," and then I asked him if I could use my own drums for the Christmas concert and he said, "Sure, good idea, just check it out with your folks," and then he shook my hand and I left.

FALCO: Great! That's terrific, Gray! And your school
   records show that you began doing better.
   What . . . Darn! Hang on a sec—tape change . . .
   Okay. Now, what about other stuff? What about
   girls, for example—what about Daisy?
GRAY: That went okay, too, for a while . . .

Ross had been kidding me about Daisy for a long
time, and once when I called Jemmy, which I'd only
done a few times, he said he was going out with this
girl, Patricia or something, and they'd been, you
know, fooling around, and I wondered what that was
like. I'd even thought about how it would be, like
maybe with Daisy, especially sometimes when I
couldn't sleep and—well, anyway, I sort of minded
that Ross kidded me about her, but I also sort of
didn't. He didn't have a girlfriend himself at first, so
I thought maybe he liked Daisy, too, but then after a
while I decided he didn't because he started hanging
around this girl named Carla in his English class.

Pretty soon he started saying I should ask Daisy
out, and finally at lunch one day he said, "So, didn't
you tell me your brother's been bugging you to go
to some party or something that church group is
having the night after the Christmas concert? There's
your chance, man. Ask her to go."

Pete *had* been bugging me about it, but it hadn't occurred to me to ask anyone, or even to go.

"Suppose I ask her and she says no?"

"That's the chance you always take with girls, don't you know that?"

"Yeah, but . . ."

"But nothing! Hell, if you don't ever ask a girl out, you'll never go out, you know?" He looked like he was trying hard not to look like he did look: proud of himself. "I asked Carla out last night."

"Yeah?" I tried to hide my surprise. Okay, envy, and maybe admiration, too. "Cool! What did she say?"

Ross grinned. "She said yes. So we're going out this weekend. And if you ask Daisy to that church party, maybe the four of us could go out after Christmas." He reached over and socked me on the arm. "I'd have asked Daisy out myself instead of Carla, only I didn't want to risk you pulling that knife on me."

I stared at him. I mean, I was pretty surprised. I hadn't talked about my knife since that first time. "What knife?" I asked, trying to look innocent.

"What knife! What are you, terminally lame? The knife you carry in your sock. You think half the school doesn't know?"

"Jeez, I haven't even *mentioned* it since you told me about the whole no-tolerance thing," I said, mad. "So how come everyone knows?"

Ross rolled his eyes. "He walks around with a knife-shaped bulge in his sock, which his pants don't always cover. And he leaves his socks on the bench in the locker room after PE while he showers, and . . ."

"Shit!" I said. "I did?"

"Yeah, you did. Yesterday. And if I hadn't put them in your locker, which you'd left open, you'd be one knife short today."

I touched my ankles together, even though I knew the knife was there. "Thanks," I said. But I was really, really embarrassed, even though I didn't mind too much that Ross knew about it.

◇ ◇ ◇

Daisy took a different bus from Ross and me, and she always sat on a stone wall away from the other girls, reading and waiting for her bus. "Go for it, man," Ross said that afternoon, pushing me toward her. "Go ask her. What can you lose?"

"She could say no."

"Sure she could. You don't have a date now, and you won't have a date then. No loss. Just the status quo. But if you ask and she says yes . . ."

"Yeah, yeah, okay."

My heart was pounding all over the place, but I tried to look as cool as Perfect Peter when I walked toward Daisy.

"Hi." I sat down next to her. The wall was cold and damp, and I wondered how she could sit on it, but then I saw she was perched not only on her coat but also on a neatly folded newspaper. "Good book?"

"It's the English book," she said. "*Romeo and Juliet.* I'm reading ahead. Have you read it?"

"No, ah, not yet. Is it any good?"

She looked amused, like that was probably a dumb question. "Yes, it's beautiful."

"It's a love story, right?" I figured that would let her know I'd at least heard of it.

"Yes. Kids our age. They fall in love, but their families are enemies."

"Not good, huh?"

"What do you think?"

"Not good. Daisy . . ."

"Whoops!" She closed the book and jumped to her feet. "There's my bus! See you—um, Gray, isn't it?"

"Yes," I called after her. "Gray Wilton!"

◯ ◯ ◯

"Not bad," Ross said when I told him. "It's a start, anyway. Try again tomorrow."

◯ ◯ ◯

The next day it was easier, and by the end of the week, she was laughing at my jokes and she'd even talked me into reading snatches of *Romeo and Juliet* out loud with her so she could practice for reading Juliet's part in class if the teacher asked her to.

"Today's the day," I said confidently to Ross one Friday morning on the bus.

"What day, man?" Ross asked sleepily. "We don't have a test, do we?"

"No."

"What, then? You're going to pull your knife on Zorro and carve up his ugly face?"

"You wish," I said, laughing. I was in a really good mood, better than I'd been in for a long time. I'd called Jemmy again and told him a little about the jock pack, mostly sort of joking and telling about Ross's and my secret entrance, and I told him about Halifax and the Christmas concert and about Daisy, too—okay, maybe I bragged a little, but heck, I figured maybe he'd been bragging himself, you know, about Patricia, or whatever her name was. Then Dad made me get off the phone and said I'd have to pay for calling Jemmy from then on and how come I had to call him anyway when the postal service still delivered mail as far as he knew, and we had a fight about his not letting me use the computer. But after a while I just tuned him out because I'd already said what I wanted to say to Jemmy anyway, and besides, I still felt really good about Ross's and my secret way into school. And I didn't want to make Dad any madder than he was, because I was still hoping he'd agree to let me take lessons from Mr. Halifax's friend after he heard me play in the Christmas concert.

So that morning I was thinking about all that, especially about how I was gonna have real music lessons. *I've got my knife, too,* I thought, *just in case. I've got Ross. And I'm gonna have Daisy.*

"Today," I announced to Ross on the bus, "is the day I'm gonna ask Daisy to go to the party, and she's gonna say yes."

Ross grinned. "Way to go, stud," he said. "Way to go! I told you it'd work. I'll ask Carla to the movies or something again today, too." He yawned and lay back in his seat, closing his eyes. "Okay." Then he opened them. "Which door we going in?"

"Basement door," I said promptly. "I don't want those jock-aliens to spoil my mood."

◯ ◯ ◯

I daydreamed through all my classes, never raising my hand, and I said politely, "I don't know, sorry," the one time I was called on. The teacher was too surprised to yell at me. After lunch, though, helicopters began whirring around in my stomach, and by dismissal I had to take deep breaths and clear my throat to make myself calm down.

"You keep drinking all that water," Ross said when I stopped at the water fountain on the way to the bus parking lot, "you're gonna have to come back in and take a piss before you ask her."

"No, I'm not," I said, but I stopped drinking anyway. "If the rest of me's as dry as my mouth is, I'll never have to piss again. Come on, let's go."

"You go, man," Ross said. "I'm not going with you. This is a solo job."

"I know that. But we can at least go outside together."

We walked to the front entrance.

"Shit," I said. The helicopters in my stomach turned to jets when I saw Zorro and his friends standing there. "I'm going out our secret door."

Ross grabbed my sleeve. "No, you're not. You go out there now, half the school will see you and we'll never be able to use that door again. Come on. We'll run past them."

He broke into a run and I followed, trying not to hear the clucking sounds the jock pack made as soon as they saw us.

Zorro and the others joined hands across the doorway when we got near them. "Hey, lookee here!" Zorro chortled. "We got some little fishes running right into our net!"

Too late, we turned, and the jock pack closed

around us. I hit out at no one in particular, and then I felt myself being yanked back. The circle had broken apart and Mr. Vee was holding me. A couple of other teachers were yelling at Zorro and company, and the JV basketball coach was holding Ross. Both of us kept trying to break free and slug those turds.

"Cool it, Wilton," Mr. Vee said to me, grabbing my arms. "It's all over."

"They ran right at us," Zorro said with this real innocent look on his ugly face. "We were just trying to stop them from falling down the steps. I don't know what got into them."

"They were waiting for us," Ross yelled furiously. "Standing there waiting for us, holding hands like they were making a—a human chain, sort of . . ."

"A net," I said. "They were making a net."

"Is this true, Baker?" one of the other teachers asked Zorro. "It's kind of hard to believe you were trying to keep them from falling, you know what I mean?"

"Well, sort of true, sir," Zorro said fake-meekly. "Just a little initiation rite we sometimes do with freshmen. You know, to toughen them up. No one was going to get hurt. They just—overreacted, is all."

I could see that the rest of the jock pack got a real kick out of that. They were grinning and trying real hard not to laugh.

"We do not permit initiations of any kind at Greenford High," the teacher said sternly.

"No?" Zorro said innocently. "Well, we didn't know that, sir. We're really sorry." He turned on the charm and smiled, first at the teachers, then at me and Ross. "Sorry, fellas," he said to us, holding out his hand. "No hard feelings?"

I stared at his hand. It was all I could do not to spit in it.

"Terrel, Wilton?" said Mr. Vee. "Shake hands, boys. That's a very gentlemanly apology."

I glanced at Ross, who shrugged and took Zorro's hand. I saw him wince in pain, so I got ready to squeeze Zorro's hand before Zorro could squeeze mine. But Zorro was faster and stronger, and I bit my tongue to keep from yelling when I felt the little bones scrape together.

By the time Ross and I finally got outside, Daisy's bus had left.

So had ours.

◇ ◇ ◇

I stayed at school late every day for Christmas-concert band practice. It was going to be this whole big-deal performance, with parents invited and everything. Mr. Halifax had given me an expanded solo part in a special arrangement of "The Little Drummer

Boy," plus lots of other great stuff, so I knew I could really show Dad, and everyone else, too, that I was pretty good, maybe even good enough for those lessons Mr. Halifax had talked about.

Anyway, after practice I usually went on just kind of jamming or working on more songs I was writing because I could do that at full volume at school, and then I could check out how the songs really sounded when I used my own drums on Saturdays. Also I knew Daisy was on the school paper and often stayed late herself. And every day I hoped she would walk by the band room and hear me. But here's a weird thing: This one day when I was working on the bass for a new song and it was going really well, I heard this noise outside the door, which I'd left open a little on purpose in case Daisy went by. When I looked up, I saw not Daisy but Zorro. And even more of a surprise, he just kind of nodded at me, said, "Cool, man!" and walked away. That made up a little for the dancing-and-drumming routine, like maybe Johnson and the others had been more to blame for that, and Zorro really respected drums after all, and maybe even respected me, too, now.

So more and more, I went on thinking it was going to be all good soon; maybe things were gonna be better in Greenford after all.

FALCO: So what happened?

GRAY: What do you think? It all fell apart, that's
what happened, like everything always does. It's
like this poem by this guy Robert-something—
Frost? Yeah, Frost. We had to read it in English.
It says good things—he calls them gold—don't
last, at least that's how I see it. Anyway, it's true
about good things not lasting. Falling apart.

FALCO: Tell me about when your good things fell
apart.

GRAY: I have to, right?

FALCO: Right.

GRAY: Well . . .

I'd been practicing on the school's drums like I said,
but they weren't good enough to really do justice to
what I had to play in the concert, which was on a
Friday night. I was sure Dad and Mom were going
to the concert, but I'd kind of put off asking Dad
about taking my drums till the last minute. See, I
knew I was going to have trouble with him about
that, and I sure was right.

I waited till breakfast the weekend before the
concert, and as soon as I asked, he said, "No," like
he didn't even have to think about it.

I kind of gulped and I could feel myself getting

hot and cold at once and getting mad, too, and I think I said something really lame like, "Huh?" because I didn't really believe what he'd said—well, I didn't want to, anyway.

"You heard me, Gray. They're too valuable and too bulky and you've been using the school's drums anyway."

I tried to sound calm because I was pretty sure that yelling wasn't going to work, and I knew I had to think of an argument he'd buy. So I took a deep breath and said, "But Dad, Mr. Halifax wants me to use my own drums. The tone's gone on the school ones, and—"

"Tone!" said Dad. "Since when do drums have tone?"

I took another deep breath, still trying to hold on to my famous temper. "Trust me, Dad, they do. And Mr. Halifax—"

"Damn your Mr. Halifax! How in hell does he expect me to get all your drums into the car?"

"Maybe you don't need to take them all." Mom looked like she knew we were about to have a huge fight. "Maybe just the snare drum. Isn't that all you need for 'The Little Drummer Boy'?"

"I do need them all, Mom." I was still being Mr. Calm, right? Trying to, anyway. "I'm using the bass for a bunch of other pieces, and I need the tom for fill."

"Well, you can use the school drums for that stuff." Dad stabbed his eggs with his fork, like it was their fault we were having this discussion and they were on my side. "It's not like you're Louis Armstrong. Stop being such a prima donna. It's just a school concert, for God's sake, not Carnegie Hall or some damn place."

That was the end of Mr. Calm. I yelled the only thing I could think of, which was "Louis Armstrong didn't play drums!" but what kept echoing in my mind was "It's just a school concert," and I was about to say something about that when Peter gave me a look and said, "I'll drive his drums to school, Dad. No problem."

"It's not the driving," said Dad. "What if something happens to the drums? They cost a small fortune, you know. I don't have the money to replace them. It was risky enough getting them here from Massachusetts in the moving van."

"Nothing's going to happen to them," Peter said soothingly, buttering toast as if that was going to calm things down. "And if it does—well, maybe insurance will pay for it."

"You have an inflated idea of insurance, Peter,"

Dad said pompously. "If something happens to them in the house, maybe. Or in the car, maybe. But at the school—"

"So what's going to happen? The band room's locked except when it's being used, isn't it, Gray?"

"Usually," I said, even though I remembered a couple of times when the last person out forgot. Another deep breath. Big swallow. *No temper,* I told myself. *No temper. Chill.* "Please, Dad? Don't you want me to sound good in the concert?"

"I'm not sure I can even go to the concert." Dad got up from the table. "I've got meetings all that day, way into the evening."

I couldn't believe he'd said that, and I think I stopped breathing, and I know his saying it knocked even the problem of my drums versus the school drums clean out of my head.

"So soon before Christmas, Harry?" Mom asked softly. "You can't skip the evening ones?"

"We'll see," he answered. "I doubt it."

"You skipped a meeting for Peter's big basketball game," I reminded him, sort of choking the words out.

"That was a Saturday meeting, Gray, not as important. And besides, it was basketball." Dad threw his napkin down and got up from the table.

My hand made a fist around my napkin, crumpling it into a ball. I was about to let myself explode again and yell out about the music lessons and everything, but very quickly, Peter put his hand over mine. "I'll get your drums to school, kid," he told me as both our parents left the room, Mom sort of scurrying after Dad. "And wild horses couldn't keep me and Mom from that concert."

I knew he was being nice and I knew I should be grateful. But that old black cloud came back and I felt like I couldn't breathe again and my throat was closing up, so I didn't thank him or even tell him why Dad *had* to go.

FALCO: That must've been awful, Gray! No wonder the black cloud came back! But wasn't that youth group party going to be around the same time? I want to hear about the concert, but what about the party? Did you ask Daisy?

GRAY: I don't much want to talk about the concert anyway . . . Yeah. Yeah, I did ask Daisy. Kind of last minute, though. I was mad at Dad all week and that's mostly what was on my mind, that and whether there'd still be some way I could get to take those lessons. But I figured at least Pete would get my drums to school for the concert and Mom would hear me play, and maybe she'd talk Dad into the lessons. But yeah, okay. Daisy. Lindsay kind of pushed me, I guess you could say . . .

"So are you going to the youth group party?" Lindsay asked me at the bus stop the day before the Christmas concert, which was going to be on that Friday, and the party was Saturday. "You don't even need a date. Plenty of the younger girls are without dates. They'll be ecstatic if there are extra boys."

I shook my head. I was still worried about the music lessons, and I really didn't want to talk about Daisy to anyone, maybe especially not to Lindsay. Lindsay meant well, but sometimes she was a little too nosy. Besides, at that point I still hadn't quite decided about asking Daisy.

"You want me to ask someone for you? Or just sound someone out? I've seen a couple of girls watching you. Daisy Jenkins for one. I think she likes you."

"No, that's okay," I said, but I felt my heart do a sort of skipping routine for a second. "Thanks anyway." Then I guess I pretty much decided I'd better make up my mind before Lindsay played matchmaker, so I said, "I'm going to ask her myself. I just haven't had a chance yet."

"Way to go!" Lindsay said with this huge grin like she really cared.

Then the bus came and puppy-dog Hannah waved at us—at Lindsay anyway—through the window. "You'd better hurry about asking her, though," Lindsay said as she sort of skipped up the bus's steps.

⬡ ⬡ ⬡

The next day, the day of the concert, was going to have to be the day. The sun was shining, which I guess helped cheer me up. No black cloud, I told myself. No jock pack, just me and Daisy. Lunchtime, I figured, as I got dressed.

I got out of the house real early without being searched, which seemed like a good start, and I helped Pete take my drums to school and unload them. Then I hung around on Vesey Street till Ross arrived on the bus. We went in the basement door as usual, and I spent my morning classes writing down cool things to say to Daisy. When the lunch bell rang I tried to ignore what was going on in my stomach. There still was no black cloud and no jock pack— and there was Daisy in the cafeteria, sitting with a bunch of other girls.

When I went up to her, they all stopped talking and looked at me like I was about to make a speech or something and they'd paid good money to hear it.

My damn tongue froze in my mouth, and I couldn't remember what I'd written down.

"Um—Daisy," I said, hoping the other girls would go away.

They didn't.

"Um, Daisy—could I talk to you a minute?"

"Sure," Daisy said. She gave me a smile.

The other girls smiled, too.

Now what?

I tried looking at the other girls, again hoping they'd finally get the idea that the table was kind of crowded for a private conversation.

But they didn't get that either.

"Maybe—maybe alone?" I suggested.

Two of the girls looked at each other and giggled.

"Oh." Daisy pushed her chair back. "Sure. Okay. Where?"

I shrugged. "Anywhere. Hall, maybe?"

"Okay."

She walked toward the hall, and I followed her, my heart pounding. I tried not to wonder if my family had a history of heart trouble.

"You're in that concert tonight, aren't you?" she asked.

That was better. Much better! "Yeah," I told her. "Drums."

"Drums are fun," Daisy said. "I like them."

"Yeah?" Better still! "I'll show you how to play if you want. Sometime."

"Sure."

By then we were standing in the hall outside the cafeteria.

"How about now?" Daisy asked. "I've finished my lunch."

"Okay." I ignored the fact that I hadn't even started mine. Then I realized that I didn't want to ignore the fact that teaching her to play wasn't what the point of this conversation was supposed to be. "No, wait," I said.

"What?"

"There's this party. At the church we go to? You know, my family. My parents go, and my brother. Me, too, most of the time. There's this youth group and they're having a party. It's tomorrow night. And I was wondering—I mean, it'll probably be really putrid, but would you like to go? It's okay if you wouldn't. You probably have something else to do anyway. And I know . . ."

Daisy laughed and touched her fingers to my lips. Her fingers felt soft and light, like feathers. "I'd love to go. What time?"

"You would?" I felt like rockets were going off inside me. I also think I might have blushed, which was pretty embarrassing. "Wow!" came bursting out of me, which must've sounded really lame, but she didn't seem to mind.

Daisy laughed again. "What time?" she repeated.

"Oh, yeah. The party starts at eight."

"And where is it?"

"Oh. Well—where do you live? Maybe I could come get you? My brother and me, that is. He can drive. I can't. Yet. You know."

"Yes, I know. I can't drive yet, either. I'm at seven fifty-six Hall Street."

"Hall Street."

"That's almost downtown from here. You go down Ridge Road and it's a left right . . . I mean a left *just* before Cross Street. Want me to write that down?" she asked as the end-of-lunch bell rang.

"Yeah, maybe you better."

"Okay." She tore a piece of paper out of her notebook and scribbled it down.

"Ridge Road to Hall Street, Hall's the left just before Cross," I read out loud from the paper.

"Mmm-hmm." She smiled at me as kids spewed out of the cafeteria. I smiled back, but then I saw Zorro's friends slinking around at the edge of the crowd, so I jammed the paper into my pocket, said, "See you!" and left quickly, trying not to look like I was in a hurry.

"About the concert?" I heard her call after me. "Good luck!"

◇ ◇ ◇

Perfect Peter gave my arm what I guess he thought was a brotherly punch that night when he let me off at school an hour before the concert, which was when anyone who was in it was supposed to be there. "Good luck, buddy." He grinned. "We'll be rooting for you."

"Yeah, thanks," I said, still kind of high from lunch period. "Thanks for the ride. And thanks again for taking the drums this morning."

"No problem. Listen, maybe Dad will show up after all."

"Yeah, and maybe the sun will rise in the middle of the night. I really don't care." That was a lie. I did care, but I'd decided if I worried about it, I wouldn't play well, and I sure didn't want to screw up even if Dad wasn't there. Maybe Mr. Halifax would be able to talk Dad into lessons even if Dad didn't hear me play—as long as I didn't screw up. At least I was going to have my own drums. "See you," I said to Peter.

"Hey!" Peter reached out again and grabbed my shoulder. "He's not such a bad guy, you know?"

"Not to you, maybe," I said. "He likes you. You're who he wants you to be." I squirmed out of Peter's grip, wanting to get away while I was still in a good mood. "And I'm who he doesn't want me to be. But so what, you know?"

"You could maybe try a little harder with him. I know he loves you, Gray. You baffle him, is all. He's worried about you, he . . ."

"No." I got out of the car and kept the passenger door open. "*He* could maybe try a little harder with me. See you later. Thanks for the ride." I shut the door—okay, maybe by then I slammed it—and ran into school, down to the music room.

Right away I could see something was wrong. Mr. Halifax and a bunch of kids were clustered around the door looking grim, like the concert had been canceled or something.

"Gray." Mr. Halifax stepped out of the crowd and came toward me. "Son, I . . ."

Suddenly everyone was staring at me, looking really tense and horrified.

"What?" I asked, bewildered. "What?"

"I don't know how anyone got in," Mr. Halifax began. "I'm sure the door was locked, and . . ."

Wham! It was like someone with iron gloves had punched me in the stomach. I pushed past Mr. Halifax and the kids into the band room.

I couldn't breathe when I saw.

There in the middle of the floor was my drum set, every drumhead slashed. Bits of Mylar lay on the floor by my battered snare drum. The bass's shell was scratched and the tom's was dented, and the stands were twisted.

I still couldn't breathe. Everything was still and sort of enlarged, like a freeze-frame in a film.

"Wow," someone behind me said in a low voice, like he was awestruck or something. "The guy who did this must've used a sledgehammer!"

The kid was trying to be sympathetic, I guess, but I couldn't react to him. His voice made the film roll again, though, but in slow motion. I kept blinking, I think, trying to put my drums, my beautiful drums, my own—soul, I guess—back together with my eyes.

But nothing changed; they stayed strewn around, twisted metal and shredded Mylar.

And still I couldn't breathe, couldn't feel anything.

For a minute it was like I floated out of myself right up to the ceiling, and I looked down on my dead drums. Then pain smashed into me as if I'd been torn and beaten like they had, and I plunged back down.

I knew who'd done it.

I heard myself say, "Zorro," under my breath, and I felt bad stuff boil up inside me with the pain.

Mr. Halifax came in and put a hand on my shoulder. "I'm afraid you'll have to use the school drums after all," he said softly. "I'm so sorry, Gray. We'll get to the bottom of this, punish whoever did it . . ."

"I know who did it," I said through clenched teeth. "I know damn well who did it."

"Well, now we can't be sure, can we, till we investigate? But when we do find out—"

"I know right now, Mr. Halifax," I said. It had to be him, had to be Zorro, and that really sucked worse than anything, because I'd thought when he'd said, "Cool, man," when he'd heard me play that he'd really liked it and maybe he was going to lay off me; maybe he even knew I wasn't some worthless piece of shit. But now I was sure he'd just been checking out the practice room so he could break into it after school and smash my drums, or, okay, maybe the school's drums—but maybe he'd seen Pete and me bringing my drums to school and knew it'd be even better to smash my own ones.

I heard myself saying, like it was someone else saying it, "When I find Zorro, I'm going to— to . . ." Then my eyes burned, like there were tears coming, so I guess I pushed Mr. Halifax away and ran through the crowd of gaping students. I ended up outside, shaking, leaning against the cold edge of the building.

Where was he? Where would Zorro be? Where did he live?

But then I pictured him and Johnson with me and Ross in the locker room that time. Even if I could find out for sure he did it—like who needed proof, but I knew the school would want that—even if I could prove that he did it, I knew he'd pulverize me if I told anyone.

And I knew he'd do the same if I confronted him about it.

"Goddamnit," I whispered. "Goddamn him!"

◯ ◯ ◯

Mr. Halifax came outside and asked me why I'd accused Zorro, but I didn't feel like, you know, analyzing it. I just blurted out, "Who else?" and then I clammed up. Nothing seemed worth anything then at that point anyway, not even going to the party with Daisy.

I got through the concert using the school drums, but it wasn't the same, and even though people clapped a lot, I knew I'd messed up a few times and that the drums had sounded pretty crummy, not even half as good as mine would've. Mr. Halifax told me afterward that it was fine, and when Mom came backstage she said the same thing, but I knew it wasn't as good as it should've been, and anyway, Dad wasn't there for Mr. Halifax to say it to. Then Mom went back into the auditorium and later, when I came out from helping stow the school drums and the other instruments in the band room, I saw Halifax talking to her, and I wondered if he was saying anything about my drums. I guess I hoped Mom hadn't noticed I was playing the school ones. I wasn't exactly eager to tell her why I'd been playing them if she *had* noticed, because I knew if I did, she'd tell Dad and all hell would break loose.

On the way home in the car, Mom said, sort of tensely, "Gray, honey, you were really great, and Mr. Halifax says he wants you to have professional lessons. Of course we'll have to ask your father—but, Gray"—she turned around and looked at me— "Gray, why didn't you tell me about your drums?"

"I don't know," I said.

She took one hand off the steering wheel and put it on my arm. "You must feel awful about them," she said, sort of carefully.

I could feel tears coming into my eyes again, so I just nodded.

"Honey, we're going to have to tell your father."

I nodded again, and she sighed and said, "Well, maybe I'll tell him later tonight, after I tell him how good you were, hmm?"

I still couldn't say anything. I was pretty sure Dad

wouldn't be impressed enough with how good I'd been to not care about the drums, but I didn't want to tell Mom that.

I was right, too.

I took Barker out when we got home, and then I took him up to my room and told him about Zorro and the drums and how Dad was going to blow a gasket, which he did. He yelled so loud he startled both of us. Barker'd been lying with his head on my chest, and I'd been rubbing his ears and talking, but when we heard Dad yell, "Goddamnit, I told him it was risky taking those drums to school!" Barker jerked his head up and I whispered, "Here it comes. Betcha he's going to yell for the next few hours."

It wasn't for a few hours and I only heard some of it, but what I heard was long enough and loud enough for me to get the gist of it. Finally I heard Mom say, "His teacher says he's very talented, Harry, don't you think . . ." Her voice trailed off, and in a few seconds Dad yelled, "Lessons! How many times do I have to tell you that it's not a good idea to encourage him in this? Music's an okay hobby, I suppose, but it's not going to earn him a living, and if he doesn't do better in school and develop some ambition, he's going to end up no better than a janitor or a grocery store clerk or in some other damn dead-end job."

Then their voices got quiet and I didn't hear any more.

◇ ◇ ◇

I stayed in my room all day Saturday with Barker, sometimes reading but mostly just, I don't know, staring at the ceiling. I had a new mantra now. It was: *Nothing's gonna change; gonna get worse, gonna get worse now, gonna get worse.*

When I said it out loud a couple of times, Barker jumped up and started licking my face and wiggling around like he was trying to make me laugh.

But I couldn't.

It was Zorro's fault I hadn't been able to play my own drums.

And it was Dad's fault I wasn't going to have those lessons.

No matter how I tried to push it away, I kept seeing pictures of that serious-plan-that-wasn't-a-plan-yet in my mind.

The knives-arrows-guns one, not the rope-and-handcuffs one.

I skipped lunch and Mom didn't bug me about it, but before dinner she came in and sat down on the bed next to me.

"Gray," she said softly, "it's terrible about your drums, really terrible. And I'm sorry about the lessons. But at least the school has drums that you can go on using, and someday maybe we'll be able to afford to get you new ones of your own. We can't now, honey, but maybe someday we can. And maybe you can save your own money for them, too, and for lessons—which you can take on your own when you get older anyway. There's no point in sulking, honey; that won't bring your drums back or change your father's mind. Now, I want you to get up and wash your face and come down to dinner, and then I want you to go to that party tonight."

"I'm not going," I said.

"Yes, Gray, you are," Mom told me. "It's not good for you to sulk like this. And besides, it would be terribly unfair to Daisy for you not to go. You have to think of her. She's probably all excited about it. What's she going to think of you if you let this business with your drums get in your way?"

Then she took hold of my hands and pulled me up.

So I went, but I was pretty sure it would be grim.

◯ ◯ ◯

For a while Daisy and I just sat kind of far apart on the sofa without talking, and we watched the other kids dance. But finally, Daisy said, "I love 'The Little Drummer Boy,'" and she actually moved closer to me on the sofa. That made me a little glad I'd gone to the party, but I still was in a pretty bad mood. I couldn't get the picture of my smashed drums out of my mind—or the one of my plan.

"You played 'The Little Drummer Boy' really great last night," Daisy went on, sort of purring. "And I could hear the bass and stuff in the other songs, too. You're so good on those drums!"

"I'm better on my own drums," I told her, and explained. I didn't say anything about the lessons, though.

Her eyes got really big and horrified. "That's awful!" she said. "I bet it *is* Zorro. He really sucks. He thinks he's, I don't know, the boss of the whole world, or something. He and those other guys, some of the girls in our class fall all over themselves to go out with them. But my friend Elena did go out with him once, and she said he was totally stupid. He spent the whole time either bragging or talking about football. I mean, she likes football, who doesn't, but they went to this really good movie and he wouldn't even talk about it for one second afterward."

Daisy's saying that made the mind pictures fade some, and I edged my arm along the back of the sofa until I was finally able to put it across her shoulders.

She didn't seem to notice, just went on talking about school, her classes, and the freshman play, which she was going to try out for after Christmas break.

Very carefully, I pulled her a little closer.

"You should try out, too, Gray." She sat up straighter, away from my arm. "You should! Would you?"

Damn! Just when I was getting somewhere. I felt my bad mood coming back again.

I shrugged. I'd never cared about being in plays. Reading bits of *Romeo and Juliet* with Daisy hadn't been too bad, but, heck, that wasn't in public. This would be!

Daisy touched my face again with her feathery fingers, like before. "I've read the play already," she said, sort of purring. "And I'm going to get the script. I'll show it to you when I get it. We could practice some of the parts together. There's this really neat part for a boy, too . . ."

Practicing together—I hadn't thought of that! For that, maybe I could stand it. *If that's what she wants,* I said to myself, *what the hell?*

So I said yes, and she let me put my arm over her shoulders again.

FALCO: That sounds promising! What about Christmas?

GRAY: Christmas. Why do they have a holiday like

that when everyone's programmed to expect
it to be perfect, so when it isn't, everyone's
miserable?

FALCO: Was everyone miserable at your house? Were
you miserable?

GRAY: Kind of, yeah . . .

I guess I'd known all along that there was no way
Mom and Dad were going to get me another drum
set for Christmas, even though I guess I kept hoping
they'd find some way to. Like a few years before, the
whole family had gotten together and paid for some
kind of fancy new saw for one of my uncles. So I
thought maybe Mom might have done something
like that to get me new drums, but I should've realized Dad would never allow it, not after the way he'd
carried on about the old ones, like it was my fault
that Zorro had trashed them, and not as long as he
felt the way he did about music anyway. Dad had
ranted for days about how he'd told me not to take
them to school—as if he hadn't pretty much said it
was okay when Peter had said he'd drive them there.

So that was one thing that wasn't perfect at
Christmas, at least not for me.

Also, after the Thanksgiving disaster, I don't
think any of us were too happy with the idea of
Christmas anyway, especially since it was going to be

just us. We were going to go to church and then to
this one aunt's, about three hours away. We did have
a tree, thanks to Pete, I guess, who came home with
it a few days before Christmas. Usually we all decorated our tree together on Christmas Eve, sort of
made a party out of it, just the four of us and Barker.
But this time Pete was going to be at the Mallers'
Christmas Eve, so we decorated the tree the day before that. Pete kept trying to make it fun, clowning
around with the ornaments and stuff, but I was still
in a shitty mood, and so was Dad, and when he and
Mom started fighting about the lights, I just went up
to my room.

On Christmas instead of coming home after
church and having a big huge breakfast with sausages
and bacon and eggs like we usually did, we just had
toast before church and then we rushed through our
own presents because we had to get to my aunt's. I
knew right away when I looked under our tree that
I wasn't getting a drum set, but I'd even hoped a little
that it might be out in the garage, but it wasn't. Mom
whispered, "Maybe next year" to me, so I guess she
knew how I felt.

I don't remember much about what I got—a
couple of CDs from Pete, though, which was okay.
But Dad gave me a book of hunting stories, like he
was still trying to make me into a young version of

himself or Pete. Mom gave me some shirts and a book about writing music, but it didn't seem to have much for drummers. Maybe she meant well, but I couldn't get too excited about it. Pete and I gave Mom and Dad the usual stuff, I guess. I don't really remember. I don't even remember shopping for anyone except Barker. I gave him a big rawhide bone and a new collar, bright red. He looked really cool in it.

FALCO: So you must have been kind of depressed on Christmas. In a bad mood.

GRAY: You can say that again!

FALCO: What about Daisy, though? Did you see her on Christmas?

GRAY: No. But the day before school started again she came over with the script of the play we were trying out for . . .

Dad even seemed to like her when she came over. But before that, when I'd told him I was trying out for a play, he said he wished I'd try out for soccer or even track instead. Then when I told him *Daisy* wanted me to try out, he actually grinned—no, leered—and said it was okay. "Good idea," he said, winking. "Maybe you've got the right instincts after all!"

Question: What if I was the kind of guy who ac-

tually liked being in plays the way I like playing
drums—the kind of guy who wanted to be in plays,
you know, professionally, like I knew by then I
wanted to play drums and write songs? I bet he
wouldn't have approved then, girl or no girl!

FALCO: No, he might not have. But go on about the
    play.
GRAY: Yeah, okay . . .

Play tryouts were after school a couple of days after
we got back from Christmas break. They were in the
GHS auditorium. Ms. Felby, the English teacher
who also did plays, didn't look anything like what I
thought a play director would look like. She had on
normal teacher-looking clothes, and the only dramatic thing about her was big gold earrings that
swayed back and forth when she stood up on the
stage and talked to all us nervous tryer-outers.

"All right, people." Her voice was as big as the
earrings, so I guess that was dramatic, too. "Let's get
started. Act One. I need two people, one to read
Kathy and one to read Joe."

Daisy poked me. "Come on," she said. "Let's
do it."

I hated it, hated to get up in front of everyone
and read out loud pretending to be some stupid dork

who was in love with a make-believe woman. But Daisy sure wasn't make-believe, and Daisy wanted to play Kathy as badly as I wanted to be her boyfriend, so I let her pull me up onto the stage and I read Joe's lines, and I don't think I stumbled very much.

But later Ms. Felby had me read Larry, a very small part that only appeared in the third act, and she had Cal Johnson—right, guess whose little brother he was?—she had Cal Johnson read Joe. Cal was huge and maybe the best-looking kid in the freshman class and an A student and on the freshman boxing team. And popular. Girls called him a hottie and guys seemed to like him, too, especially the baby freshmen jocks.

I knew even then that I was toast, and I was right. When the cast list went up the next afternoon, Daisy'd gotten Kathy and Cal Johnson had gotten Joe. My name wasn't on the list at all. So much for my theatrical career, right? I didn't care about that, but I did care about Daisy, and I knew if Cal got the part, I'd sure be in trouble with her. It was one more bad thing, like nothing good could really last. I told myself I should try to snap out of the bad mood that crashed in on me, but I wasn't sure how this time, and I didn't feel like talking to anyone except Barker, not even Ross or Jemmy, not that I could afford to pay for calling Jemmy anyway. So I decided to walk home.

It was snowing very lightly, the kind of snow Barker had loved as a puppy and still did love. He liked to snap at snowflakes as if they were flies.

Why'd Dad have to make him a hunting dog, anyway, I thought for the millionth time.

Does Barker know that the ducks he brings back to Dad are dead?

Yeah, I answered myself, scuffing the snow with my boot; *yeah, he probably does.*

Does Barker know I'm dead? If anyone does, he does.

I could feel my bad mood spiraling then, spiraling black-cloud mood, and I looked around at the snow, which was so new it was white and pure like I figured I sure wasn't, and I began feeling I couldn't breathe again. I tried dumb things, whistling, kicking snowy stones ahead of me, running—but as soon as I did that, I slipped and splatted down on the side of the road.

For a few minutes I just stayed there. It was kind of peaceful, with the snow falling quietly on my face, gently, like Daisy's fingers, but cold. White snow, pure snow, I kept thinking; snow doesn't have to do anything, go anywhere, prove anything. *Hello snow, can I be you?*

Might as well be, I thought. *Can't do sports, can't study. Can't keep my own drums from being trashed. Can't fight Zorro. Can't be Perfect Peter. Can't get my own father to like me. Can't like him. Can't even get into a stupid school play.*

Whoa, Gray, cut it out, I said to myself. *What a wuss! Crybaby, crying in your beer, like Dad would say. Snap out of it, he'd say. Right, snow?*

I must be crazy, I thought, sitting up. *Talking to snow!*

"Good-bye, snow," I said to it, out loud this time, and stood up.

But I was still in the same stupid mood.

Maybe I'll never be any different, I thought. *Maybe this is who I really am. Maybe this is a forever mood.*

I tried to scoop up enough snow for a snowball, but even that didn't work. Instead I picked up rocks and threw them at trees as I passed them, but that didn't help much either. Then when I got to my street, I saw Lindsay outside her house, sweeping snow off her front walk.

"Damn!" I said under my breath, and I ducked into my driveway fast, but she'd seen me. She waved and then called, "Missed you on the bus! Ross didn't know why you weren't there." She put down her broom and ran across both our yards to me. Her cheeks were pink from the cold and her eyes looked worried. "Everything okay?" she asked.

No, I screamed inside, *no, nothing's okay!* But out loud I said, "Yeah, sure. Everything's great."

She looked so closely at me, I felt like a germ or something under a microscope. "You don't look okay," she said softly. "What's the matter? Did the cast list go up for the freshman play?"

"Yeah," I said lightly, like it didn't matter.

"And? . . . Oh, Gray!"

"'Oh, Gray' what? So I didn't get a part. I really didn't want one anyway."

"Maybe you could do something backstage. You know, lights, props, moving scenery around."

"Yeah. Yeah, I guess."

"That can be a lot of fun," she went on enthusiastically. "I did costumes for my freshman play. It was neat. The play was, you know, historical, so I got to alter lots of fancy old dresses." She laughed. "Some of them were so old they smelled. A funny smell, like mothballs and sweat mixed."

"Yeah, cool. Well, nice talking to you," I said. "I've got to go in. Homework." I started to go, but then I turned back. I really didn't want to be crummy to her. "Um, thanks," I said.

Mom and Dad should've had a girl the first time, I thought as I went inside. *A girl like Lindsay.*

Instead of Perfect Peter.

◇ ◇ ◇

Things didn't get any better that night. Mom gave me a funny look when I went inside, and when Dad came home, I heard her talking to him for a while. Then he called up to my room, "Gray, come down here a minute."

Mom was sitting at the kitchen table, looking worried and scared, and Dad was standing near the sink, looking tense and mad.

Mom smiled, sort of, and motioned me to sit down, but Dad jumped right in, so I didn't bother to sit.

"Your mother said the school called. Some woman called Throckmorton . . ."

"The guidance counselor," Mom explained softly, as if I didn't know. Self-esteem, remember?

"Ms. Throckmorton wants to talk to you," Dad said. "She thinks you were having trouble with some of the older boys before Christmas break. Even before the drum incident. Is that true?" He made it sound like an accusation, like she'd really said, "Your son's been caught stealing from the office," or, "Gray's cheated on his last seven tests."

My stomach felt weird, almost like the jock pack was standing in front of me. "What kind of trouble?" I asked carefully. I couldn't believe we were really going to talk about it.

"Why don't you tell me?"

"Trouble like at Parker," Mom said timidly.

Shit, I thought. *Okay. So it's my fault, right? Never*

mind Zorro and company. "I haven't pulled any knives, if that's what you mean," I told them. *Or guns,* I said to myself silently.

Both my parents were looking at me funny.

"No, no, honey." Mom glanced up at Dad. "I just meant—well, at Parker there were those boys who teased you . . ."

". . . and you promised you wouldn't ever do anything stupid like you did there no matter what anyone said to you," Dad said. "We agreed that fistfights are okay if the other guy starts it, but weapons . . ."

"I didn't tell Ms. Throckmorton that your father checks your pack for—you know," Mom said. "But we know you haven't taken anything like that to school—have you?"

Something about that made me want to laugh. I mean if she *knew* I hadn't taken "anything like that" to school, why was she asking if I had? But I figured maybe she was smart enough to know Dad wasn't all that clever at searching, and that maybe he'd missed something. Not that she'd dare say that to his face, though.

Meanwhile, they went on with the conversation they were having with each other, like they really didn't need me to contribute.

"We're not blaming you, honey," Mom said finally, like she'd noticed me again. "Your father and I want to help. But we also want to make sure you don't get into trouble yourself by retaliating the wrong way if someone *is* being mean to you."

"Like I told you back at Parker," Dad said, "there are bullies everywhere. What you have to do is not give anyone any reason to bully you. Bullies like to go after guys they can push around. Don't let anyone think they can do that to you, and you'll be fine. Go out for a sport like your brother instead of playing those stu— Those computer games. Wrestling, boxing, any tough individual sport if you don't want to go out for a team. A team sport would be better, of course, and your brother can tell you there's nothing like it, nothing like the friends you'll make, either, but I had a roommate in college who was a wrestler and he did fine for himself. Made some good friends with the other wrestlers and no one messed with him. Built up his body, too. You could stand a little of that, you know."

I had to struggle to keep from laughing. What did I tell you he'd say?

"Let it be known that you're tough," Dad went on, "even though you play in the band and write songs. Tell the guys that you hunt with me and Pete, for instance. Laugh it off if some jerk calls you names; don't let them get a rise out of you. But if it gets really bad, fight back. Give as good as you get, but with fists, Gray. That's all any real guy really needs."

Sure, I thought, *like in a war, that's all a "real guy" needs. Soldiers, cops; I guess they're not real guys. What a revelation!*

Dad was still talking. "And don't be so damn sensitive! That's what gets you into trouble in the first place." He gave me a thump on the back. "Okay, son? Got it?"

Ah. Must be my turn, I realized. "Okay," I said. "Right. Got it."

Dad smiled. "See?" he said to Mom. "There's no reason for him to see that guidance person. He can get all the guidance he needs right here at home. You come to me, Gray, if there's anything you can't handle. Like those drums; if you find out for sure that that kid trashed them, I'll sue. And remember, all bullies are cowards . . ."

He went on for a while about that and with a repeat of one of his favorite stories about how he'd been teased as a kid because his dad got fired from some job or other and about how he'd built himself up by lifting weights and learning to box and playing football, and by the time he'd finished talking, he'd convinced himself that everything was going to be just fine.

Mom didn't look so sure, but as usual she didn't argue with him.

And neither did I, not after all that.

FALCO: So did you go to see the guidance counselor?
GRAY: Yeah. Yeah I went to see her. I guess Dad
    didn't tell her I could get all the guidance I
    needed at home, or she didn't believe him,
    because she called me in anyway . . .

Ms. Throckmorton was sitting at this big desk with a huge heap of papers on it, and she had her back to a window that had a jungle of plants on the sill. She had on a bright yellow jacket, and I remember thinking maybe she dressed that way to cheer people up. I figured anyone who went to see a guidance counselor would probably be feeling pretty crummy.

"Hi, Grayson," she said. "Have a seat. Sure is cold today, isn't it?"

That kind of surprised me because I hadn't really noticed, but I said, "Yeah," anyway.

"I hope we're not going to have one of those really cold winters. Do you like winter? Snow? Skiing and skating, things like that?"

Whoa, I thought. *She sure does switch to personal stuff fast.*

"Not really," I said. But then I told her about

Barker and the snow and our game with the snow-balls. I thought that would be pretty harmless.

"Dogs are great," she said. "I had a yellow Lab when I was growing up. Snitch, his name was, because he used to steal food if we left it out."

"Barker doesn't do that," I told her, and then felt kind of dumb. I mean, that was harmless, too, but, hey, she hadn't called me in to talk about dogs.

Then she got down to business.

"Grayson," she said, "how do you feel about Greenford High? How does it compare to your old school"—she looked at a couple of the papers she had in front of her—"Parker Middle School, in Massachusetts?"

"Greenford's okay," I said, figuring I ought to be polite, and then wondering if the papers she had on her desk said anything about Suspensions One and Two. "Bigger than Parker." Then I remembered that supposedly Parker didn't send behavior records to high schools, so I relaxed a little.

"Friendlier?" she asked. "Or the same? Or less friendly?"

By then I'd lost track of whether she was asking about Parker or Greenford, so I said, "About the same."

"So you must've found some friends here, right?"

"Right."

"Gray, remember those self-esteem questions from that assembly back when school started?"

I nodded.

"Do you remember what you put on your list?"

Yes, I did, and no, I wasn't about to tell her if she didn't know, and I figured she didn't since she'd said it was confidential and since I hadn't put my name on mine. "No," I said.

"Hmmm. Too bad. Well, what's the best thing about Grayson Wilton?"

I thought of saying, "My name?" or, "My left elbow," or, "My amazing personality," or some other weird thing like that, but I knew that would probably get me in trouble, so I said, "I don't know."

Which was true, actually, the way I felt then. Besides, I still wasn't sure if playing drums or shooting arrows into targets, which I actually hadn't done for months anyway, were the kinds of things she meant.

She didn't react, which I thought was a little weird.

"Grayson," she said then, "we want every student to be happy here at GHS. We don't want anyone to feel left out of things or nervous about things or to have trouble with any of the other students. Have you had any trouble with other students?"

Here it is, I thought. *And my job is to make it go away—fast. Much as I'd sort of like to tell her.*

Yeah, and die.

"No," I said.

So then she hits me with, "Mr. Halifax says you think Eugene Baker—Zorro—smashed your drums. Could you tell me why you think that?"

All of a sudden my mouth got so dry I probably couldn't've talked even if I'd wanted to. So I just sat there. But she kept asking, so finally I said, "Well, once he kind of teased me about drumming, so I thought at first he might have done it, but I guess no one saw him or anything."

She nodded like she agreed and then she asked me to describe the teasing, so I told her about the bump-and-grind thing outside the music room. I left out the part about Zorro making me dance, but I wondered if Halifax had told her about it, since he'd seen it. Maybe not that part, though.

Throckmorton just sort of smiled and said, "That doesn't seem so very bad. Maybe he just meant to be funny!"

Man, I thought, *what's the use?*

When she let me go, Zorro was waiting outside her door.

FALCO: Did you ever find out what Zorro went to her about?

GRAY: Not right away, no.

FALCO: Well, what happened next, then?

GRAY: Maybe we could skip that part?

FALCO: No, Gray.

GRAY: Yeah, I knew you'd say that. But I bet you're not going to like it.

FALCO: Try me.

GRAY: Well, you asked, remember? Okay . . .

That Saturday there was more snow. I was getting used to my lousy mood, kind of like a stray animal following me around. Mom asked me to shovel again. Peter and Lindsay were off skating. Dad went out . . .

FALCO: Yes? Gray? Come on!

GRAY: Yeah, okay. Okay . . .

Dad went out to a gun show, and when Peter said he was going out with Lindsay and Hannah and Hannah's boyfriend, Dad grumbled that "no one" wanted to go with him.

Yeah, well, he didn't check with me. *Damn,* I thought, shoveling snow. *I should've offered to go.*

And I started picturing it in my mind. I mean, I'd never been to a gun show, but I thought there'd be lots of long tables with different kinds of guns on them, and guys standing around hefting them, peering down their sights, whatever.

Should get me a gun, I thought, really thinking it this time, and wondering if I could get one if I went to a gun show. I decided probably not, but I wondered if I could get Dad to get me one. *Maybe he would,* I thought. *Maybe he'd even already wanted to. And then . . .*

I tried not to take that idea much further.

Luckily, Mom opened the front door then and Barker came bounding out of the house. "Watch him?" Mom called. "I'm making a cake and he wants to play."

"Yeah, okay." I tossed a handful of snow toward him, and he jumped up trying to catch it, but it was loosely packed and it shattered. Barker looked surprised as usual at the vanishing snow, and that made me laugh.

"Hey, Barker," I said, "want to play ice ball?"

Barker, true to his name, barked.

I made an ice ball and threw it as far as I could across my yard and the Mallers'. Barker took off, ears flapping, sniffed where it landed, dug in the new snow till he found it, and brought it proudly back.

"Good boy." I rubbed Barker's ears. Then I hugged him, burying my face for a moment in his doggy-smelling hair. "Good boy," I whispered. "Good Barker." I straightened up. "Man's best friend, huh?" I said.

Barker sat, panting, eyes expectant.

"Yeah," I said. "Man's best friend. Mine, anyway. You don't care, do you, Barker? You don't care if I'm not Perfect Peter. Right now you just care"—I made another ice ball—"if I can throw far enough for you to get some fun out of chasing." I threw the ice ball, and while snow began falling harder, covering the path, I kept on throwing till Mom came to the door again and Barker ran up the front steps. "Thanks for watching him," she called, letting him in. "Cake's in the oven. Heavens, Gray, I thought you were shoveling the path!"

"I did shovel it," I called back. "Then it snowed more."

"Well, shovel it again, then. Please," she added, and went back inside.

So I shoveled some more and when I was done, I went to Ross's and we did what we usually did, sat in front of his computer.

"Got 'im!"

That was Ross.

"Got 'im!"

That was me.

We were offing different enemies this time, mega-weird ones that strutted like jock clones in their tight green body armor, but we had guns that burned it, turned it red-hot and then white-hot.

"That one's Zorro—you get him!"

I did.

"You're getting better."

"Better? Man, I never miss!"

Ross looked at me sort of sideways. "You did once or twice. Before."

"Never," I said.

A bunch of green-armored clones sashayed into view, like they owned the world.

"The jock pack!" we both yelled, and I opened fire.

◯ ⬡ ◯

"Look what I got," Dad announced when he rolled in at suppertime that night. He pulled a shiny handgun out of a bag and showed it to us almost before he was in the door, stamping snow off his boots and grinning like he'd just won a million bucks in the lottery.

I couldn't stop staring at it. It was small enough for him to hold in one big hand, but it had a clip that looked as if it could hold a lot of rounds.

"Isn't she a beauty?" Dad said.

"If a gun can be a beauty," Mom said drily. "Or a she."

"Oh, come on, Samantha! It's a semiautomatic, boys," he said to me and Peter—proudly, like he'd made it himself. "From Germany." He rubbed his fingers lovingly over its shiny surface. "World War Two. Beautifully—no, perfectly—restored. It even"— he put his hand in the bag again and pulled out a box—"came with ammo, and it shoots like a dream. It'll be the star of my collection." He put the gun down on the kitchen table and shucked off his jacket, throwing it onto a chair. "I'm going to make a special stand for it," he added, opening the fridge and taking out a beer. "Display it as it deserves to be displayed. I'll let you guys shoot it tomorrow if it doesn't snow, okay?"

"Sure, Dad, thanks," Peter said.

"Yeah," I said; I was still staring at the gun. It was as if it and I were connected, and I knew how. It was like an answer to a prayer, and it also scared the hell out of me, excited-scared, though, like, I don't know, those eagles were back flying around in my stomach again, I guess.

"Thanks, Dad," I said, and for once I really meant it.

◇ ◇ ◇

The next day, after church and Sunday dinner, Dad actually delivered. He showed us how the gun worked, and he had Peter shoot first. After a couple of rounds Pete finally hit the target, but not the bull's-eye.

"It takes a while, son," Dad said. "Handgun's different from a shotgun, after all."

"Sure is," Peter said.

"Practice makes perfect," Dad told him.

Peter laughed. "I'm not sure I really want to practice with it. I think I'll stick to hunting. But it sure is a beauty, Dad."

"Isn't it? Your turn, Gray . . ."

I took the gun. Its silver-blue metal was cold in my hand, but it felt good, and again I had the weird but this time nice feeling of floating up out of my body and looking down at myself holding it. That looked good, too—oh, it looked very good! The gun was a little large; my hands were smaller than Dad's and Pete's, but it fit me well enough, and it was so much more compact, so much less clumsy than the shotgun. I hefted it, feeling its weight. It was comfortable, safe, reassuring, easily part of me, part of the boy I was looking down on and watching. . . .

"Neat, huh?" Dad said.

I smiled at him, which was the first time in quite a while I'd felt like doing that. "Yeah," I said. "Yeah, it's neat."

I lifted the gun with both hands the way Dad demonstrated, lined it up with the target, and squeezed the trigger, firing shot after shot dead center. Bull's-eye, bull's-eye, bull's-eye.

Dad and Perfect Peter looked at me with—what? Could it have been respect? Admiration?

"Wow," said Peter. "I guess we know who the real marksman is in the family!"

"Nice shooting, Gray," Dad said, but he sounded stiff, like he was disappointed. "Very nice." He held out his hand for the gun.

Is that all you can say? I thought as I gave it back to him.

But I knew it was, knew Dad had wanted Peter to be the one to take to the gun instantly, to fire round after round into the bull's-eye.

And then I knew for sure that someday I'd show both of them, and everyone else, just how good I could be.

Someday soon.

Would I?

FALCO: You want to say any more about that now?
GRAY: No.
FALCO: Okay. We'll come back to it. So—meanwhile, how were things with Zorro after you'd both seen Ms. Throckmorton? Any repercussions?
GRAY: Yeah. Oh, yeah . . .

I was going past the art room on my way to lunch the Monday after Dad showed us his new gun, mind-ing my own business like I always did, when this arm shot out and grabbed me. Before I knew it, I was in the art room with the door shut, and Johnson and Zorro were glaring at me like I was supposed to know why.

I guess I did, though, at least my stomach did, because it sort of lurched, but I just said, "What?" anyway.

"You know what," Zorro said right in my face. "You little snake. I was beginning to think maybe you were okay, but my pal here, Johnson, he was right. He warned me about sneaky little kids like you."

I squirmed around to see if there was any way I could get away from him, but Johnson was blocking the door and Zorro had this iron grip on my neck. Johnson came closer and twisted my arms behind my back.

"Okay, sing," Zorro said. "What did you say to Throckmorton about your stupid drums?"

I decided the best thing to say would be nothing, so that's what I said.

Zorro shook me.

"What did you say to her?" His voice was low and his words were like icicles, and his finger was jabbing at my face. "You said I trashed your stupid drums, didn't you?"

"Everyone knows," Johnson said, sort of sneering, "that if you accuse a person of something like that, you have to have proof. Which you don't. No one saw who did it. That includes you. Right?"

It still seemed like a good idea not to say anything.

Johnson poked me in the chest. "Hey, something wrong with your tongue? You can talk—you're human, right? One of the higher animals, although probably a pretty low form?"

Zorro laughed. "Yeah, a pretty low form." He got serious again. "But I've heard him talk, so at least he's, like, humanoid." He grinned at me and shook me by the neck. "So, humanoid, isn't that right? Didn't you tell that lie to Throckmorton? Hmmm? Hmmm?"

I still didn't say anything, and Johnson went over to one of the tables and picked up this jar that was half full of black paint. While I was having this sinking feeling about what he was going to do with it, he screwed the top off and held the jar right against my chin. I couldn't even move my head away because of Zorro's hand behind my neck. I could feel a couple of his fingers pressing on the back of my head.

At least, I thought, *it doesn't look like he's going to throw it at me.*

You know how school art room paint smells? It's not a bad smell; I even used to kind of like it. I was just thinking that I was glad it wasn't oil paint or something like that when Zorro said, "Talk! Talk or drink," and he put the edge of the jar against my mouth.

My stomach squinched and I almost wished he'd thrown it after all. No way did I want to drink the paint, but I sure wasn't going to tell him I'd squealed on him, sort of, to Throckmorton, by saying I'd told her I'd thought at first he might have done it.

Johnson laughed and grabbed a brush. "Let's give him a taste, see what he looks like with black lips." He dipped the brush in the paint and Zorro moved the jar a little and Johnson painted my lips with the paint.

It was sort of thick and cold and gooey, and suddenly I didn't like the smell so much anymore.

"Talk, you little humanoid worm," Zorro whispered. His whisper was weird, like something out of a horror movie maybe, which was what I felt I was in right about then. "Talk, talk, talk. Count of three," he said, loud now. "One. Two. Three!" And then he moved his one hand all the way up to the back of my head and with the other hand he put the jar against my mouth. I clamped my lips and teeth shut, but Johnson dug his fingers into my jaw joint so I had to open up, and Zorro poured thick black paint down my throat while I choked and tried not to swallow.

As soon as he moved the jar away I began barfing.

Zorro said, "Jesus!" and shoved a wastebasket over to me and I bent over it, barfing black paint and I guess whatever was left of breakfast, and still choking, too, while Zorro and Johnson laughed. "Guess that'll teach you to squeal," said Johnson. "Plenty of paint in here, and my dad's got some really good rat poison if we need it."

Then I heard Zorro say, "Wrong room; it's main lunch anyway and besides, the art teacher's out sick," and I realized someone had come in. By then my stomach was hurting really bad and I was trying to keep tears from sliding down my face, so I didn't realize who it was till this girl's voice said, "Are you okay?" and I realized it was Lindsay Maller.

She put her arm around me, and I wanted to either run away or stay there next to her, but how could I? So I wiggled free and managed to sort of croak, "Sure. I'm fine. I like doing this." There was black-paint barf all over my shirt and I tried to wipe it off, which of course meant then there was black-paint barf on my hands, too.

"Yeah, he's fine, whoever you are," Johnson said. "Something he ate, I guess."

Zorro and he both laughed.

I couldn't resist looking right at him and saying, "No, something I *drank,* thanks to you."

Lindsay looked at the empty jar and gasped and said, "You didn't actually make him *drink* that, did you?"

Zorro put on his innocent face like he had that time on the steps and said, "Who, us?"

"Nah, he just likes paint," Johnson said. "Just had a little too much." He nodded at Zorro and Zorro smiled, and they both moved closer to Lindsay, who put her arm around me again, barfy shirt and all, shoving me out the door and down the hall, which was pretty deserted because it was still the main lunch period. She took me into an empty room, sat me down at a desk, sat at the one next to it, and handed me a bunch of tissues from the purse she'd been carrying. "Gray?" she said, only it was more like a question. "Maybe you'd better see the nurse?"

I was feeling pretty horrible and smelling horrible, too, and I began wondering if art room paint is any kind of poison, but mostly I just wanted to go someplace by myself to clean up and let my stomach stop burning and churning, so I shook my head and wiped my hands and my shirt with the tissues.

"Do you want me to find Peter?"

God no, I thought, and gave her another head shake.

"What happened?"

Now how was I going to tell her that?

"Gray . . ."

"You saw," I said, trying not to barf again from the taste in my mouth, and wondering what to do with the barfy tissues. "They made me drink paint."

"Yes, but why, Gray? Why?" She held out her hand for the used tissues like everyone's mom does no matter how awful the tissues are.

I gave them to her. "Must be how they get their kicks."

Lindsay took the tissues over to a wastebasket near the teacher's desk and dropped them in. Without turning around she said, "Is Zorro the guy who gave you the black eye last fall?"

Whoa, this girl's sharp, I thought, staring at her— blankly, I hoped, as she came back to me.

"Let's go to the principal," she said. "Come on."

There was no way that was a good idea. "No," I said.

"But, Gray, they're—"

Okay, I kind of lost it then. "No, Lindsay," I said. "No, no, no, no, no!" I ran out of the room so fast I bumped into Hannah, who was coming in, and I ran through the halls, down to the basement, and found an unlocked storeroom near Ross's and my secret entrance and I went into it and banged my fists against the walls until they hurt worse than my stomach. Then I made myself into a little ball, and I think I cried, and I know I wanted Barker to be there.

FALCO: I'd have wanted that, too.

GRAY: Yeah?

FALCO: Yeah. I'd have been mad and hurt and embarrassed. How about you?

GRAY: I guess.

FALCO: Did you tell anyone? Mr. Halifax, Ms. Throckmorton?

GRAY: Are you kidding? I mean, man, telling's what the whole stupid thing was about!

FALCO: Did you tell Ross?

GRAY: Yeah, sure. He said he'd never use black paint again. Nice, and it sort of made me laugh, but not much help, you know?

FALCO: What about Lindsay? Did she do anything, tell anyone?

GRAY: Maybe. I don't know. I think she told Pete, at least they had a fight and I think it was about that . . .

I felt too crummy that night to notice much of anything; mostly I just stayed in my room. But I could hear Pete slamming around in his room, and the next day he ran to school instead of taking the bus. Lindsay pretty much ignored me after giving me a weak smile and asking if I was feeling better, and her friend Hannah sort of stared. That went on for days. Pete and Lindsay didn't talk on the phone, which they'd been doing almost every night. But when Pete started taking the bus again, Lindsay wouldn't even look at him. So finally I asked him what was going on and he just said, "We had a fight, okay?" I asked him what it was about and he kind of spat out, "None of your business, weirdo!" like he was mad. But then that night he came into my room.

He kind of stood there for a few minutes, looking at my books and CDs and posters and stuff—looking at everything except me.

"Excuse me, sir," I said finally. "I don't want to interrupt, but the museum closes at nine."

He kind of laughed then and gave me a Dad-type punch on the arm. Then he sat down on my bed and said, "Okay, listen. This is kind of awkward and weird, but I guess it'd be better to say it than to keep wondering about it. Lindsay told me she saw Zorro and his friend making you drink paint in the art room."

It was like something switched off inside me, and all I said was, "So?"

"Well, so did it happen?"

"Maybe."

"Oh, come on, Gray, did it?"

"What if it did?"

"Well, okay, *if* it did, do you want me to do anything about it?"

"No."

"That's what I thought, but Lindsay thought you might want me to. Jesus, paint! Were you sick?"

"*If* it happened, yeah, I was sick."

"Those bastards."

"Yeah."

He got up and looked out the window toward the Mallers' house. It was dark out, but I knew Lindsay's light was on because I'd seen it go on earlier. At least I was pretty sure it was her light.

"Gray," Pete said, "I don't want to interfere or play the big brother or anything, and I know you want to take care of your own business, but—"

"What business?" I said. "Everything's fine."

"Yeah, right! Then how come you've been moping around and how come the black eye in November when I was sick and how come your grades went south last quarter and—"

"They're better now. At least they were for a while."

"Okay, that's great. Or it will be if you keep it

up. But how come the guidance counselor wanted to see you and how come—"

"The museum," I told him, "is closed."

He looked like I'd hit him.

We stared at each other for a few minutes and I thought of a million things to say, and I bet he did, too, but we didn't say any of them, and finally he left.

FALCO: Sounds like he was trying to help, but I guess
   you weren't ready for anyone to do that, hmm?
GRAY: I guess.
FALCO: So how were things after that?
GRAY: Pete and Lindsay made up a week or so later,
   and he didn't bother me anymore. Neither did
   she or anyone else.
FALCO: And you? What did you do?
GRAY: Do? I dunno. I guess I just went along, you
   know, trying to avoid Zorro. Every time I passed
   him in the hall, he made drinking motions, you
   know, pretended to be lifting a glass—no,
   whoops, a paint jar—to his mouth, and making
   drinking noises. Pretty soon the whole jock pack
   did the same thing anytime they saw me. I went
   back to trying to ignore them. Mostly I thought
   about Daisy and tried to study, you know? But
   sometimes everything got to me and I just kind
   of couldn't.

FALCO: Tell me about Daisy.

GRAY: I didn't see much of her around then because
she was in that play, you know, rehearsing.
Still . . .

Daisy was the best thing that had happened to me so
far all year, the only really good thing—well, maybe
except for Ross, too—and I couldn't wait till the play
was over so she'd have time to go out with me. They
rehearsed only once a week at first, but after a while
it seemed like they were rehearsing all the time, she
and Cal anyway. Cal, Johnson's brother, remember?
Once after the "glub-glub" drinking routine, Johnson
grabbed my arm and said, "I got a message for you,
Crater Face. Quit bothering Daisy Jenkins. She
doesn't like it. You're annoying her, you little turd."

But I didn't believe him, that Daisy didn't like it.
I knew she was busy with rehearsals, and that Cal
was, too, so I was trying to make sure she didn't forget about me. I'd been making sure to find her in the
halls at school and we'd smile and say hi, and I kept
telling her how good she looked. She did, too; she'd
started wearing a little makeup on her eyes, I think,
and her hair was loose instead of in braids, and she'd
started going around with a different bunch of girls,
the real popular ones. I knew she couldn't go out with
me or anything because she usually had to rehearse

after school and sometimes on weekends with Cal or with the whole cast. And I knew she was too busy most of the time to answer the notes I put in her locker, what with rehearsing and keeping up with her grades and the paper and whatever else she was doing. But I also knew she didn't mind and that she still liked me, because she'd write quick answers like, "Thanks for the math tip," or, "Sorry, can't meet you after school. Rehearsal"—stuff like that.

When it got to be February I began thinking about getting her a valentine, and Ross wanted to get one for Carla, so one day we went to this big stationery store in what passed for beautiful downtown Greenford.

"Here's one." Ross came around the edge of a card rack and handed me a valentine that was just a big heart with lace drawn around it and a takeoff on the usual "Roses are red" poem. "Nice and feminine, you know? Just like Daisy." He winked.

I'm like, "*Blagh.* Would you give it to Carla?"

"Okay, no. But I already got one for her." He held up a paper bag.

"Yeah? So what's it like?"

He shrugged. "It's got dogs on it. She likes dogs."

I grinned. "Puppy love, huh?"

Ross's face got red and he punched my arm. I laughed and punched him back, just playing around.

But then this scrawny saleslady with a sour, pinched face comes down the aisle and says, "Boys! No roughhousing or you're outta here."

So we both put on real serious looks and Ross says, "Yes, ma'am," and I go, "We're real sorry," and Ross is like, "We're picking out valentines for our girlfriends."

Scrawny-face rolls her eyes and says, "Well, do it quietly," and she leaves.

So we grubbed around more for a while without finding anything, and I stayed up half that night trying to make a card and wishing that Jemmy, who could draw, was around. But I figured maybe he'd be busy making a card for his own girlfriend, the one he'd been fooling around with, or said he'd been, anyway.

Besides, I wanted to do Daisy's myself.

I wanted it to be something that would make her smile and feel good and know I was waiting for her.

Man, was I waiting!

Sometimes I imagined what it would be like to lie down someplace soft with her and just hold her. Maybe outdoors someplace in the sun. Just hold her and touch her hair. Okay, maybe touch more than that if she'd let me, but I wasn't sure she would, at least not right away. But if we could just start with that . . .

And if I could just talk to her. She understood about Zorro, she liked my drumming, she liked *me*.

I remembered that she always signed her notes with a little daisy drawing, and that gave me an idea. I must've thrown away half a package of construction paper getting it right, but it looked pretty good when I was done. I cut lots of little daisies out of white paper and gave them yellow centers with marker and pasted them on yellow construction paper and drew green stems and leaves on them. I made one of them way bigger and better than the others and put it in the middle, and then near it, but sort of in the background, I made a skinny made-up flower, maybe sort of a tulip but in the shape of a heart. And inside the card I wrote "To the best Daisy in the world. Be my valentine?"

I signed it "GW," and on Valentine's Day I slipped it through the vent in her locker, where I put my notes. Oh, yeah, and I wrote "7 MORE DAYS!" on the envelope. It was that long till the last performance of the play, and I figured I'd write a note every day from then on to say how many more days.

And then the play would be over, Cal Johnson would be toast, and I could have Daisy all to myself.

◯ ◯ ◯

The play was on a Friday and Saturday. Just about everyone's parents, I guess, went to it the second night. Everyone said that the second performance would be better than the first one, so I went Saturday, too, pretty sure that was when Daisy would want me there.

She was great. So was Cal, I guess, but he had this long kiss with her that made me squirm. I knew it was just a play, but I was surprised Ms. Felby let Cal go on that long with a kiss in a school play. I figured maybe she hadn't in rehearsals, but Cal sure drew it out in the performance I saw.

Anyway, everyone clapped loudest for Daisy and Cal. So did I, but it was all for Daisy. Then I went backstage. It was mobbed, like everyone was looking for someone and handing out flowers and hugging people who had goo all over their faces and their costumes half off, and everyone was talking excitedly about the performance: "So good! . . ." "I never thought they'd . . ." ". . . third act . . ." ". . . Daisy and Cal especially . . ." "I loved the part where . . ."

I pushed past everyone, picturing walking out of there with Daisy while Zorro, who I'd seen in the back of the auditorium, watched enviously, and while Johnson looked surprised that I'd beat out his little brother.

Finally I looked through an open door and saw Daisy sitting at a long table with a couple of other girls. She had a huge towel over her shoulders and was rubbing makeup off her face with a handful of tissues.

She looked happy and excited; her face was all pink and I could hear her laughing at something one of the other girls said. So I went in and yelled, "Daisy! You were great! Really, really great! The best!"

She turned around, holding the soggy tissues in her hand. "You think so?" she said eagerly. "Thank you. It was so fun, Gray. I wish you'd been in it."

"Yeah, me, too." I shoved past a couple of kids till I stood right behind her. "But, hey, if I'd been in it, I wouldn't have seen you in it, you know?"

She laughed, a bright ripple of a sound, but the girl next to her rolled her eyes.

Well, so what, I thought. *Who cares?*

I put my hand on her arm. "So let's go out, you know, get something to eat, whatever, as soon as you're ready, okay? We could walk to the corner and . . ."

But Daisy was shaking her head sort of vaguely and waving out the door to someone who was just coming out of another room—the boys' dressing room, I figured. It was Cal, damnit.

"Oh, Gray, thanks, but Cal and I are going to the cast party. Thanks anyway."

"What?" But I'd heard her.

She said it again, *"Cal and I,"* like they were a pair already just because of one stupid onstage kiss.

Then it hit me that they'd all *have* to go to the cast party. I mean it was *for* them, so of course they'd all have to go. So I sort of cleared my throat and said, "Hey, why don't I come, too? To the cast party? I was, like, almost in the play, and . . ."

The girl next to Daisy did laugh this time, and she prodded the girl next to her with her elbow and whispered to her. The other girl laughed, too.

Daisy scowled at them and hissed, *"Shhh!"* Then she said, "No, Gray, I'm sorry, it's really just for the cast and crew. And . . ."

Cal came over then, real casual, like he didn't give a damn, except he had this smirk on his face that I wanted to smash. A few blobs of makeup still colored his hairline and his neck. I was trying to think of what I could say about that when he said, "And she's going with me, Crater Face." He put his arm around her. "So butt out."

She seemed to like it, his arm, I mean. She sort of snuggled against him and smiled.

I felt like I'd burst if I didn't hit him. I could feel my fists balling up like they were doing it without me telling them to. But like I said, Cal was huge, with gigantic muscles; he'd pulverize me, I knew. So I just looked at him and said, "You've still got makeup on. Looks good on you."

That, of course, was a mistake. Big time.

"Want some, fag?" Cal said. "You all out of it or something? Amazing—I didn't think a fag'd ever run out—"

"Shh, Cal." Daisy tugged at Cal's arm. "That's mean. Come on, let's go." She put down the tissues and stood up. The towel fell off and I saw that she'd already changed into her regular clothes.

"Yeah, let's," he said. "The air in here's kind of close. Out of our way, Crater Face."

Before I could say anything, Cal put his hand in the center of my chest and pushed. He caught me off guard, you know? I sprawled right into a knot of kids that I guess had been watching, and I fell flat on my butt while Cal and Daisy left the room and everyone else stood around and laughed.

FALCO: What did you do?

GRAY: Shit, what do you think? I got up and left.

FALCO: And?

GRAY: Man, don't you ever let up?

FALCO: Do you need a break? Maybe we should stop for today. The hard part's coming, right?

GRAY: Yeah. Right. A hard part, anyway . . . Okay. Let's get it over. I went home and—and I took Barker out for a run . . .

It was dark, cold, really late; there was slushy snow on the sides of the road but not in it; cool air rushing past, Barker running beside me, both of us speeding ahead. My butt still hurt, but running was working the kinks out some. Who needs Daisy anyway, I tried to tell myself. Little bitch; she'd never said she was *going* with Cal; she'd never said anything like that all the times I'd asked her out. "I've got a rehearsal," that's what she'd always said when she refused, or, "I've got to catch up on homework"—not, "I've got a date," which was probably what the truth was. Yeah, one time after school she was at the coffee shop with a bunch of other cast members and Cal was next to her, sitting close, smiling into her eyes, flirting—the scumbag! *He's no better than his brother,* I thought; GHS is full of power-hungry jocks like Johnson and Zorro and stuck-up bastards like Cal who think they're so great, better than anyone else, better than God, probably. Stuck-up bastards . . .

Suddenly I heard something and I looked around, still running. I saw it then.

I saw a car . . . coming fast . . . rounding the corner . . . tires squealing . . . funny license plate . . . DON something . . . the headlights caught me, caught Barker . . . Barker ran on the outside; I ran onto the shoulder to give him room . . .

The car swerved and there was a thud, a sound I'll never forget. The car vanished, laughter pouring through its open windows. Barker's no longer beside me. . . .

I run back. My heart's trying to get out of my chest, my throat is tight, hurting; I can't breathe. I find Barker, but he's not moving, his eyes don't see me, they don't see anything . . .

He wasn't breathing. There was no breathing—no breath in either of us. . . .

The laughter stayed in my ears as I carried him home.

FALCO: God, Gray . . .

GRAY: Yeah, well . . . Okay. It's all right, man, it's over, you know?

FALCO: Let's take that break . . . I just have to change the tape . . . There. Now let's break for a bit.

GRAY: Nah, let's go on. Get the rest of it over with now, you know? I'm sick of the whole thing, everything. Yeah, let's go on.

FALCO: Okay, but—are you sure?

GRAY: Yeah. Yeah, I'm sure. So I—I took him home . . .

When I walked in the door, carrying him, Mom and Dad both came rushing out of the living room, like they'd been waiting for me, and Pete was there, too. Dad started yelling before he even saw me, but I just sort of held Barker out and I think I was probably crying, and Barker was all limp but with no blood or anything on him.

And everyone stopped yelling for a minute and just stared.

Then Mom said, "Oh, God, no!" in a really little voice, almost a whisper, and Dad grabbed Barker out of my arms, and Pete said, "Shit!" and put his arm around me.

Dad bent his head down against Barker like he was listening for a heartbeat and then he laid Barker down on the floor, real gently, like he was still alive but just sleeping. Dad stayed there for a minute with his head bent and we all just kind of waited.

And then he turned around, and his face was all white and sort of—what's the word?—contorted? Yeah, contorted. I think that's it.

And he said, "What in the hell were you doing taking him out running in the middle of the goddamn night? I thought you were going to a party with that girl, that Daisy."

"He came home, Harry," Mom said, putting her hand on his arm. "He came home instead and said he was going running. He told me . . ."

"Another guy took Daisy to the party," I said. "So I went out for a run. I'm sorry, Dad."

I meant it, too. I was sorry even for Dad right then. I knew how he felt about Barker. I sort of thought we'd both feel the same way, since we were the two who loved Barker best. I told him what had happened and that I was sure it was Zorro and Johnson, and I told him the license plate was DON-something.

Dad kept staring at me, shaking his head like it was all my fault and there was no way he was ever going to forgive me.

"You irresponsible jerk!" he yelled as soon as I was done explaining. "Why couldn't the car have hit . . ."

"Harry!" Mom shouted, interrupting fast. "Harry, stop! Gray's just as upset as you are. It was an accident."

"Yeah," Pete said. "It wasn't Gray's fault, Dad." Pete went on saying other stuff, but by then I was halfway up the stairs to my room and I didn't hear any more. I took Barker's picture off my bureau and I lay down on the bed with it, and I thought about playing in the snow with him and training him to do all the right dog things and cleaning up after him when he was a puppy, and playing ball with him. My throat ached like there was fire in it, but I couldn't even cry. And I just stayed there all night like I was frozen inside.

◯ ◯ ◯

The next day, Mom kept knocking on my door and coming in and sometimes bringing me food, but I didn't eat it. She talked to me, but I don't remember what she said. I don't think I even heard her.

I was still lying on my bed with Barker's picture next to me when there was another knock on my door. Then I heard, "Gray? Gray, it's me, Lindsay. Can I come in?"

I didn't really care, so I didn't say anything, and she came in.

"Gray, I'm so sorry," she said. "He was a wonderful dog. Such a good friend to you."

I didn't look at her. I looked at the ceiling. I decided not to hear her anymore.

But she picked up the picture and looked at it. "He was handsome, too," she said. "I bet you could have this framed. Mind if I sit down?"

After a while, not sitting, she said, "I'm glad he didn't suffer. I'm glad it was quick. And it's awful that whoever hit him didn't stop. Maybe they didn't even know, though, maybe . . ."

I looked at her then, I looked right at her eyes,

and I don't know why, but she gave a sort of gasp and reached out her hand like she was going to touch me. She muttered something that sounded like "God" and "Your eyes," but I was dead inside, and I still don't know what she meant. And then she left.

◇ ◇ ◇

After Barker was gone, the spiraling black cloud was tight around me again, holding me inside it, suffocating me. It was always there from then on, always. Nothing worked anymore, not even music, not even when I played Third Wheel as loud as I could when no one was home. Sometimes I took some cushions down to my old practice room in the cellar and slept there. Or tried to. Sometimes I just stared at Dad's gun cabinet and at his new handgun on its fancy stand. Or I sat on the floor or walked around in my empty drum room, drumming on the walls with my hands. Mom kept trying to make me go back upstairs but I wouldn't. My mind was sort of blank most of the time, like an empty space without any thoughts or mind pictures in it.

I didn't want to feel like that, I really didn't. I wanted to feel like I could breathe again, and think, but I didn't know what to do to make the black cloud go away. I didn't know what to do to be normal, either. I guess I'd never known. I knew my own drums wouldn't help anymore, even if I had them back again, whole. Nothing was worth anything, not even the picture of Barker that Peter and Lindsay had blown up and framed for me. It was upstairs in my old room. It was nice of them, but a picture isn't a dog.

Dad kept at me to remember more of that license plate, but I couldn't. I couldn't even remember seeing the rest of it. I thought that maybe if I saw it again, I'd remember, but there didn't seem to be much chance that I would. Dad wanted to sue whoever it was, but I didn't care about that. Even if it was Zorro and Johnson, and I was sure it was, suing wouldn't bring Barker back.

School sucked, so I didn't go. For a couple of days I told everyone I'd rather walk than take the bus, and I went down to the end of the block and waited around the corner till the bus had gone. Then after Mom and Dad left for work, I went back inside again to my practice room.

One night Ms. Throckmorton called and asked why I hadn't been in school, and after that, Dad stood outside every day till I was really on the bus, so I had to go.

On the bus the first day I took it, Ross was like, "Man, I'm sorry. That's a real bummer about your dog. Who did it?"

I couldn't answer at first, but finally I managed to

say, "Zorro and Johnson, I'm pretty sure. They were laughing, driving fast."

That afternoon I got away from Mr. Halifax and Ms. Throckmorton, both of whom said they wanted to talk to me, and I went to Ross's house and we shot terrorists or alien mutants or something from a new game he had. It didn't matter what they were supposed to be; we named them "Zorro" and "Johnson" and "dog killers" and "jock-pack murderers."

"I'm gonna do it sometime for real," I said to him all of a sudden. It just came out of me, and the black cloud moved away a little, but Ross laughed like it was a joke. He also looked at me like he thought shooting computer enemies was helping, but it wasn't, and I decided not to do it anymore. It was so fake, a kids' game. Ross just didn't get it.

Every time I saw a dog on the street I scared myself, for I wanted to kill it. What right did it have to be alive when Barker was dead?

What right did Zorro have, either?

Interlude

Juvenile Detention Center

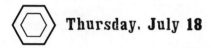 **Thursday, July 18**

Hexagons.

Gray traced five invisible ones on the wall, putting an invisible letter in the center of each one:

Z

R

D

H

L

He hesitated, then traced a sixth. He added:

G

Making a gun out of his hand, he pointed at each invisible figure.

"Pow,"

he whispered.

"Pow."
"Pow."
"Pow."
"Pow."

Then, louder, aiming into the sixth invisible hexagon, he added,

"POW!"

And finally, he turned over onto his stomach, and, making as little noise as possible, he wept.

The End

FALCO: So, Gray, it says here that your dad found out that Zorro's stepfather had a car with vanity plates saying "DONSAUTO," which was the name of the body shop he owned, and that he tried to talk to Zorro's stepfather about Barker and that they ended up yelling at each other. And that he called his lawyer and said he wanted to file charges. Is that right?

GRAY: Yeah, sure, I guess so. I didn't pay much attention to it. Barker was dead, you know? Nothing was going to bring him back.

FALCO: And things really fell apart for you at that point, didn't they? Your marks continued going down and you didn't even go to band anymore, right? Your teachers said you were "seriously depressed." Is that true? Were you?

GRAY: Yeah, I guess. It was all pretty grim.

FALCO: But you did continue going to school, anyway, that spring, right, once you went back after Ms. Throckmorton called?

GRAY: Yeah. Wish I hadn't.

FALCO: Ms. Throckmorton says you wouldn't talk to her and that your parents wouldn't, either. Right?

GRAY: Hey, you been talking to them? My teachers, Throckmorton?

FALCO: Yes. I have to see you from all sides, Gray, as much as possible.

GRAY: Yeah, well, I'm the side that knows me best, man!

FALCO: You've certainly let me know a lot about yourself, Gray, and that's helping a lot—helping *you*, remember. Now—how about answering my question? Is it true that neither you nor your parents would talk to Ms. Throckmorton?

GRAY: Yeah. Yeah, it is. She made me go to her office, and the teachers did, too, a few times, and Throckmorton asked me a lot of dumb questions, but I didn't say anything. There wasn't any point, you know? Nothing was gonna change. Nothing.

FALCO: What about your parents?

GRAY: They had a fight about seeing her, I think. Anyway, they didn't go. At least I don't think they did.

FALCO: And the really bad stuff went down in May, right?

GRAY: Do you have to ask about that? Isn't it all in
that report you have, you know, from the cops?
And in the newspapers. "Rampage at GHS"—I
remember that! Big headline and lots of lies.

FALCO: Oh? What lies?

GRAY: Shit, I don't know. Like in that clipping you
read to me. It was months ago. Who cares?

FALCO: I do . . . Come on, Gray, don't wiggle out of
it now. I need to hear what you have to say
about it.

GRAY: Yeah, but there's lots I don't remember.

FALCO: That's okay. What *do* you remember? Like
about the other newspaper stories?

GRAY: Well, they made it sound like I hated
everyone at GHS, Daisy, Ross—even Hannah,
who I didn't even know. Even Lindsay. Shit—
Lindsay! But they made it sound like I hated
all of them and like I really meant to hurt them
and like I was some kind of nut. They didn't
explain about the varsity guys, except just that
there'd been "locker-room horseplay." I sure
remember that—"horseplay"—and that Mr. Vee
had told them he didn't think there was any
stuff going on at GHS that was worse than at
any other school, that boys will be boys, that
kind of crap.

FALCO: It's too bad that you didn't tell Mr. Vee or anyone else some of the stuff you've been telling me.

GRAY: Shit, how could I? Like I've said a million times, I'd have been dead meat if I'd told, and besides, who'd have believed me? And if they had, they wouldn't have done anything, not to the varsity guys, everyone's heroes. You know that! Haven't you heard anything I've said? Man, what's the use? What's the goddamn use! . . .

FALCO: Shh, Gray. Easy, son. I *do* hear, and I do believe you. The truth's going to come out at your trial. We'll let the judge know the whole story. That's why I've needed you to talk to me and to Dr. Bowen . . . Now, look, we've got to finish this. I need to hear what you have to say about the rest of it. Why don't you just talk, just tell me what happened in the spring? April? May? . . . Just talk, Gray, just talk.

GRAY: Can I stop then? After May? Man, I'm sick of this, you know?

FALCO: Yes, probably. For a while anyway . . . Okay, Gray. Back to work. Think back to April. You were going to school again then, right?

GRAY: April? Yeah, well . . .

Yeah, I was going to school again then, but I didn't speak to anyone. I minded my own business, like three little monkey figures Mom had that she called See No Evil, Hear No Evil, and Speak No Evil. I guess it kind of bugged my teachers, and it didn't do my average any good, but I wasn't doing homework then anyway. Teachers—Wallace and Halifax especially, and even Blanchard, from homeroom—kept bugging me about it, but I just gave them the silent treatment, and finally to shut them up I said, "Yeah, okay, I'll try," but I didn't do it. Like I said, they made me see Throckmorton a few times, and the principal, too, but I wouldn't say anything to them, either. I guess everyone finally gave up, because after a few weeks they left me alone. Zorro and Johnson gave me and Ross, me especially, black looks in the halls and sometimes shoved us around a little, but mostly they left us alone, too, like they were bored with us, or maybe it had something to do with the lawyer stuff, I don't know. So it could almost have been a good time, but it wasn't. I guess it was too late for that. . . .

FALCO: Gray? Go on.
GRAY: This part's pretty bad. I don't know . . .
FALCO: You can tell me, son.

GRAY: It's—disgusting.

FALCO: That's okay—not okay that it's disgusting,
    okay that you can tell me. Maybe it'll help your
    case, Gray . . . Come on, son. I'm a lawyer, I
    don't shock easily. I've heard a lot of disgusting
    stuff. Embarrassing stuff, too. I've—

GRAY: Okay, okay . . .

So one day—I guess it was May by then . . . Yeah, of
course it was—one day, like I always did after PE, I
silently stripped off my shirt and my shorts and my
underwear and dropped them on the same bench
Ross dropped his on, and I headed quickly to my
usual vacant shower.

But then Zorro struts into the locker room, and
it's like the air changes. He gets to the shower before
I do and plants himself in front of it.

The eagles fly back into my stomach.

"What're you staring at, Crater Face?" he snarls.

"What's to stare at?" I answer. It's hard to speak,
since, like I said, I hadn't been talking much to anyone. But my brain seems to remember, and it seems
to think I should answer, so my mouth goes, "Nothing. Just waiting to get into the shower."

Ross comes up behind me, a towel around his
waist.

"Outta here, you guys," Zorro says to the few

other members of our PE class who are still in the locker room. "We got business to do here. Out."

The other kids flee.

"So, you queers gonna shower together?"

I feel Ross bristle. *Chill,* I say to myself. *Stay cool.* But I can feel that might not last.

"Hey, Johnson," Zorro calls, and then I see several jock-pack guys standing near the lockers. Like they're stalking something, they move closer. "Lookee here," Zorro says. "Crater Face and Camouflage Girl here are gonna shower together. Cute, huh?"

Johnson saunters over. "What a cute couple! Pee Wee Pecker and his faggy friend Camouflage Girl."

"Pee Wee Pecker and Pee Wee Prick," Zorro says, snapping the towel off Ross. He laughs when Ross quickly puts his hands in front of his privates.

"What'll you bet Pee Wee Pecker sucks Pee Wee Prick's dick?"

I don't want to be there anymore, but I guess I am, because I feel my stomach slide down to my ankles. I look over at Ross; his eyes are terrified, and his hands are fists, but they're still protecting his dick, and his face is red. My hands make fists, too. *Good hands,* I tell them. *Atta hands.*

Zorro's gang moves closer. In a second there's a half circle around me and Ross, cutting us off from everywhere but the shower. I act; I don't decide to,

I just do it. Like I grab Ross's wrist and I ignore his attempt to yank free, and I pull him into the nearest shower. "Come on, man," I whisper. "Maybe if we turn the water on . . ."

But it doesn't work. I feel someone—Zorro, I'm pretty sure—seize the back of my neck and jerk me out of the stall. I feel Ross being wrenched out with me, and I see, like it's a nasty ballet, the circle of boys moving to block our path to the showers.

"I hear you still think we ran over your stupid dog, Crater Face," Zorro snarls. "Your dad's lawyer called my stepfather about it. I need to hear you say I didn't go near your damn dog."

From somewhere, my voice comes out again. I wonder where. "I'm not going to say that," it says. "You did run him over."

"You couldn't have seen me in the dark, nerd."

"Yeah?" my voice says calmly. "Well, you just admitted you ran him over by saying that. I never said when it happened."

"Everyone knows it was at night," Johnson says. "Your brother told the whole school way back when it happened. So if it was night, you couldn't have seen who it was. We just want to make sure no one makes any false accusations about anyone. Any *more* false accusations."

"Let's see you do it, Crater Face," Zorro says, and the other guys take up the chant: *Do it, do it, do it!*

"Do what?" I ask, filling in for my voice this time. But somewhere inside I know what he means, and I feel sick. "Not tell? How can not doing something be doing something?"

Zorro pushes me down to my knees while Johnson grabs Ross and holds him facing me.

"Do what you've been wanting to do," Zorro says. "Suck his dick, Crater Face."

"Yeah, suck his dick," another boy says. "Maybe it'll get bigger, you know?"

There is a loud guffaw, during which I can't look up at Ross and during which I think *This can't be happening,* and during which I try to practice invisibility again, but of course that doesn't work.

"Yeah, Crater Face, pull it real hard. He'll thank you for it if it stretches."

Ross begins to squirm. "Don't you dare," he whispers to me.

As if I want to! I think, as Zorro pushes my head toward Ross's crotch, closer, burying it there. I clamp my mouth shut so hard my jaw aches. I try to hold my breath, too.

"Come on, Crater Face, open up," Zorro croons softly. "You know you want it, you both want it."

Ross's hand shoots out, somehow freeing itself from the grip that holds him, and his fist catches the side of my head, hard. This surprises everyone, especially me, and while the others are being surprised, I manage to stand up and wrench my arms free. I guess I'm trying to hit back. I don't know why Ross is hitting me, *me* of all people. Doesn't he *know* I don't want to do this? Something sort of snaps inside me and suddenly I hate him. Why doesn't he get it? Why isn't he friend enough to know I'd never do that to him? And then both of us are free and the other guys are cheering us on, yelling, "Fag fight! Fag fight!" and laughing.

I don't want to do that, either. I don't want to fight, I don't want to hit Ross. I want to run away, but Ross is hitting me and Zorro is keeping up a running commentary, but all I really hear are the names: Crater Face, Pee Wee Pecker, Pee Wee Prick, Pee Wee Dick, fag, fag, fag. I think maybe tears are rolling down my cheeks, because my cheeks feel wet. Finally I just punch without knowing who or what I'm hitting, or if I'm hitting anything, and I feel my body and my face taking the blows that Ross rains down on me, but I don't feel the pain that I'll feel later, and I hate Ross, hate Zorro, hate Johnson and the others.

Myself, too.

I hated my worthless, stupid self, too, only I didn't think that then, but I did later, much, much later, after . . .

After everything.

FALCO: Go on.

GRAY: No.

FALCO: Gray! It's important. You have to. Skip ahead if you want, skip to the day it all happened. What did you do first that day?

GRAY: I—I didn't, I . . .

FALCO: Yes, you did, Gray.

GRAY: No, I—you don't understand.

FALCO: Try me. What don't I understand?

GRAY: I wasn't there, Mr. Falco. I swear I wasn't there! I mean, it was like I wasn't there, like maybe I wasn't even me. See, that's another thing that wasn't in those stupid cop reports or in the newspaper. I mean, okay, like yeah, I was there, but I was watching. You know. Floating again. Outside myself . . . Crazy, huh?

FALCO: I think it's called dissociation. It's normal sometimes, like—oh, during a crisis, like maybe a car accident, any time when a person's under terrible stress . . . It's okay, son. Tell me what you saw when you were floating. When did it start?

GRAY: Normal, huh?

FALCO: Yes, I'd say so, under stress. What did you
    see? When did you start floating?

GRAY: Wait, I don't know. Um, dawn, maybe? When
    I got up the next day, maybe right after I went
    outside. Maybe before, maybe when I woke up.
    Yeah, then . . .

It was still dark when I woke up—not black dark;
gray dark, like right before the sun comes up. I could
see gray light around my window shade, and I felt, I
don't know, different, stronger. The black cloud was
thinner, and I knew it was thinner because this was
a special day, the day I'd been waiting for even when
I hadn't known I was. It was like I didn't have to decide anything anymore; it was all decided and it was
like my legs got me out of bed without me making
them move. I was light, free, and I got my pack from
my desk and took it downstairs and loaded up and
went outside. Light, I was so light!

I went out with my pack on like I was going to
school, and I *was* going to school, but not to class,
and I remember that made me laugh a little.

So light. Still. I was so light.

Suddenly I drift up till I can watch myself. Only
it was more like it was some other boy, some other
boy standing there, watching the sun come up, going
down the steps, hiding behind a bush when a car

goes by and a long, sweatshirt-covered arm throws a newspaper onto the house's front steps. The house is my house, I know, but I don't feel like it is.

I'm still floating, watching myself, watching the boy who is me walk down the front path, and somehow I can tell his mouth is dry and his heart is beating fast, but I don't really feel them myself. I watch him stop when he gets to the street and he looks back at the house where there's a slightly open upstairs window, which is his parents'—my parents'—room, but I don't know why he stands there looking at it. He crosses the lawn, and I remember thinking he must be glad that he won't have to cut the grass anymore.

I feel good. Gently, I float down and walk to school slowly, no need to hurry, it's still early. The sky is turning a sort of milky blue and there are birds flying around. Sometimes I float up again and I think it would be nice to be a bird. When I get to school I head for the basement door, which I know will be unlocked, ready for the morning food-delivery truck that will come a little later. But I float up when a blue sedan pulls into the parking lot and stops. I crouch behind the stone wall where Daisy sat, and I watch the principal get out of the car and go to the main entrance. He unlocks it and goes inside. I know he will go to his office and start working as if this is a normal day.

But it isn't.

I float down again. My legs ache from squatting behind the wall. I touch the knife in my sock and move my shoulders under the heavy weight in my pack. I am excited, light as air, happy, strong, stronger than anyone, than Zorro, than Dad, and I laugh as I push open the basement door and I think, *It's good; it will be all good soon, at last.*

I wait for the right time in that little basement storeroom. And I review the Plan over and over again, the Plan that I'd started to make months earlier, the Plan that I wasn't sure I'd ever do, but I'd been keeping it, working on it, just in case. This is the time, and I know that I have to do it. I'm not really hiding in the storeroom now, not in the same way I did the last time I was there. I'm just waiting. The black cloud is gone and I still feel good.

Bells ring and I can hear kids going back and forth to classes. Like lemmings, I remember thinking, little rodents running to their doom in the sea. I wait in the storeroom till lunchtime, and then before the bell rings, I go up the stairs and wait on the landing while the lemmings spill out of their classes. I take Dad's fancy handgun out of my pack and I stand there with it, waiting, waiting for the right moment, and I swallow hard to slow the pulse in my throat.

But I know my hand is steady, and I can ignore the pounding of my heart.

Suddenly someone shouts, "Look!" and the noise stops and now everyone's looking up at me, even Zorro, even Johnson, looking at me like I'm super-boy, and I feel myself smiling. I see a girl, Hannah, Lindsay's puppy-dog friend, with her mouth open like an O but no sound seems to be coming out, and that's really funny, so I laugh. And near her is Daisy, my not-girlfriend, and she yells something, but I can't hear her or read her lips, and anyway, it's too late for whatever she has to say. I see Fitz and Mor-ris sort of huddled together, staring. I don't see Cal, which is too bad, and I do see Peter, right near the foot of the stairs, but he breaks away from the other kids and runs down the corridor like he's scared.

I'm not sure if I'm glad he's running away or not; I'm not sure about Peter.

Where is Ross? Suddenly I'm not sure about him, either.

Maybe I am.

There's a noise on the stairs above and behind me and I turn my head and see Lindsay Maller running toward me like she's crazy and not afraid of me, and she goes, "Gray. Please don't do this. You don't mean it. Gray, you don't . . ."

But I do mean it. For once Lindsay's wrong, and I know I have to shut her up; she's spoiling it. So I whirl around and I point the gun at her, to scare her. I'm not going to shoot, not at her. She holds her hand up like a cop, and I hear the kids whispering below me in the hall and I hear doors opening and, damnit, I know I have to do my stuff fast if I'm going to do it at all, so I yell, "Get out of here! I don't want to hurt you! You—Lindsay—get out of here!" I reach for her and our hands touch, and then I grab her and she struggles and I twist her around and push her out of the way. I turn back again and start aiming and shooting, and right away I get Zorro smack in his ugly face and I yell "Yes!" and I feel great and strong and free like I've won after all. I've gotten him, the bastard.

Then I see Daisy running toward someone—Cal, I think—so I aim at him and fire, but I don't see what happens. Everything's loud and messy now, and confusing, and some teachers are running into the hall, so I just start shooting without aiming because I know I have to work fast, and what the hell, I know they all laughed at me, most of them, anyway, one time or another, and now they're all seeing what I can do. They're screaming and some of them are crying and running in all directions like a lot of bugs when you lift an old board or something, and it's kind of funny, like a cartoon, so I laugh while I'm shooting. Hannah runs and I guess a bullet hits her, because she twirls around and then falls and I see red bursting out like a flower on her perfect white blouse. Then I see Ross and Fitz and Morris and they're yelling stuff at me, and then Ross falls down and I see he's on the floor next to Lindsay who I guess must have decided to lie down to be out of the way, and I think *Good, Lindsay, that's smart, that's cool.* Then I see blood on her. I decide it must be Ross's blood.

There are lots more screams and shouts and yells, and then someone grabs me from behind and I see it's Peter who's grabbed me. I try to fight him like Ross tried to fight me in the locker room, but Peter wrestles me to the floor. He straddles me, he takes the gun, and everyone cheers, at least the ones who aren't screaming or who aren't dead. *Shit,* I think, and I grab Peter's arm, the one holding the gun, and I try to get it back, but he's too strong, and as I float up again, I hear a voice sobbing, "Kill me, kill me!" The voice sounds like mine, and I float down again, mad at Peter because the plan was that I'd put the gun in my mouth at the end and pull the trigger. That was going to be my invisibility potion; I'd be invisible then, finally, and who knows, I figured maybe I'd even see Barker again. Shit! I was supposed to, you know, go out with a bang that people would talk about at my funeral and in the papers, and say stuff like, "He wasn't a wuss or a fag or anything; he was strong, a real guy," and damnit, I'm still mad as hell that didn't happen!

FALCO: Gray? . . . And then?

GRAY: What?

FALCO: What happened then?

GRAY: Huh? Man, that's not important. It's over. Who cares?

FALCO: I do. Come on, Gray, just a little more. How did you get here, for instance, how did you get to be in this cell? Fill me in. Peter's still holding you down, go back to that.

GRAY: Then can we stop this?

FALCO: Yes. I promise. Peter's . . .

Yeah, he's still holding me and I can hear people moaning and crying and ambulances coming and police. Kids are lying on the floor and there's lots of blood, but I can't see who's dead and who's hurt and whether I got the right ones or not. But I'm pretty sure I did get Zorro and maybe Daisy, too, or Cal. But Johnson; I start worrying about Johnson, because I can't see him anywhere. I try looking around, but then some cops yank me away from Peter and handcuff me and take me away, and I spend all night in a smelly cell with a hard bench to sleep on, and there's a toilet without a lid out in the open where everyone can see and can laugh at you. They take your belt away and your shoelaces because they think you might try to off yourself, which you can damn well bet I'd have done right there on the stairs like I'd planned if it hadn't been for my dear brother.

Yeah.

And then the next day in the courtroom, at what they called my arraignment, Dad wouldn't look at me and Mom was crying without making a sound. This guy got up and said, "Four counts of murder," to a judge. "Counts" sounded funny and I laughed. It wasn't even people anymore, which I figured was because they were dead. Then the guy listed the dead people and it was Zorro and Daisy, like I'd thought, and Lindsay's friend Hannah, who I didn't mean to shoot, and Ross, who I didn't know if I meant to shoot or not, but probably not, even though I was still a little mad at him. No one said anything about Johnson or Cal or Lindsay, and I was mad that I obviously didn't get Johnson or Cal, but I was glad Lindsay was okay. Well, that's what I thought, anyway. Then the guy said, "And one count of assault with intent to murder," and I thought that probably meant someone was still alive but hurt, and I hoped it was Johnson or Cal, and I hoped whichever one it turned out to be was going to die. I was surprised I hadn't hit more people, but I knew I would've if Perfect Peter hadn't gotten to me when he did.

Afterward, Dad came to see me—that was the only time he did, too, at least he hasn't come again yet. He told me Lindsay was the one count of assault and she was still alive. Then he said, "Your brother's in love with her. You almost killed your brother's girlfriend, the girl he says he thinks he wants to marry someday. Maybe you *have* killed her. She's in critical condition." I said, "Fuck that!" because I didn't want Lindsay to die and also because it hit me then that Johnson wasn't even hurt, and neither was Cal. That's when I saw that the whole thing really went all wrong, with mostly the wrong people hit and me still alive, and I felt that old black cloud coming back again.

As usual, Dad didn't give a damn what I felt. He didn't even notice. He looked like he wanted to hit me, but he couldn't because there was a glass thing between us and we were talking through a hole that was covered with some kind of plastic with littler holes in it that made our voices muffled.

Dad kept glaring at me and saying stuff like "You've ruined this family" and "You've almost killed your mother. You've broken her heart."

I tuned out and didn't say anything, and pretty soon he shut up and left.

All I could think was, *I'm still here, I failed.* That's when I realized they'll just have to finish the job for me, the cops and the judge and the jury. Whoever decides, anyway.

Oh, yeah, then later on some guard showed me a newspaper story about everyone's funerals. The paper gave them four whole big pages, with pictures and everything—Daisy and Ross and Hannah and even Zorro. There was a lot about how everyone loved them and that they all did great things in school and church, like they were all really wonderful, special hero-kids, especially Zorro, of course. And there were pictures of their parents crying and their grand-parents, too, and brothers and sisters and aunts and uncles and even teachers. There were quotes from lots of those people about how terrible it was about the kids that were dead and what a loss they were, and how young and innocent they were, *blah, blah, blah.* Yeah, and there was a picture of Daisy and Cal in the play, and in the article they quoted Cal as saying, "I don't know why he shot her. I think he even went out with her once. Maybe he was jealous."

Yeah, maybe.

There was a picture of the whole damn varsity football team in black armbands and another one of

Johnson in church making some kind of speech about Zorro. One of the articles said the school was going to put up a memorial to everyone who was killed. And there was a picture of the hall where I did it, with flowers and teddy bears and stuff all over the bottom of the stairs I stood on. There was even a separate article about how Throckmorton and other counselor-type people—"grief counselors," I think they called them—were going to be around for anyone who wanted to talk.

And there was a picture of Lindsay, with an article about how she was in critical conditon and had been dating the brother of the "alleged shooter." Pete wasn't "available for comment," it said, but he was spending all his time at the hospital, and the article went on about how he's an honor student and the one who "finally subdued" me, "saving countless others from death and injury."

So Peter was a big hero. Still is, I guess.

Mostly all the whole four pages said about me was stuff like the stuff you read me before: that I'm the "alleged shooter"—not even that I'm the real one—and that I'm "in custody." Then it went on about me being "a loner who likes violent video games"—as if I played them all the time, which I didn't—and it said I'm going to be tried, maybe as a kid and maybe as an adult.

And that's it. In a while Dad had them give me you for my lawyer and they put me in a better jail—this one that's for kids, but it's still crummy. Like I said, that's it, and that's all I have to say, except to tell you that all I care about, damnit, is would they please fry me and do it fast because the whole damn plan went wrong and nothing's sure gonna get better now, ever.

FALCO: They won't "fry" you, Gray. They can't do that to kids . . . Are you sorry, Gray? Sorry about what happened, about what you did?

GRAY: Sorry? About what happened? Some of it, sure. Parker Middle. The jock pack at GHS. My dad. About what *I* did? No! Man, I had to do it. Even though it went wrong, I had to do something, you know? No one else would. No one. What else could I have done?

FALCO: What about Lindsay? What if she dies? Would you be sorry about that?

GRAY: Damnit, man, she won't die! She can't. It was an accident.

FALCO: Accidents can kill, Gray. Would you be sorry if she did die? What if she's crippled for life, something like that?

GRAY: I told you, man, she'll be fine.

FALCO: What about Hannah? She *did* die, and she didn't do anything to hurt you, did she?

GRAY: She got in the way! She must've. That was an accident, too.

FALCO: How about Ross? How about Daisy? . . . Gray? . . .

GRAY: Shit, man, shut up, can't you?

FALCO: Think about it, Gray. Between now and your trial, try to think about what you've done, who you've hurt, what their families must be feeling, what the newspaper said about all the relatives crying. Think about Barker, Gray, what you felt when he was killed. That's how those families must be feeling, don't you think?

GRAY: Shit! Would you . . . Just shut up, man, shut up about Barker!

FALCO: I'm not really talking about Barker. Just think about what I've said, son. Gray . . .

GRAY: Don't touch me!

FALCO: Okay. I'm sorry. Easy, son! Easy . . . Okay, I'll go now. Listen, thank you for talking to me as much as you did. You've helped a lot. Now I'd better go to my office and work on how I'm going to defend you. I'll be in touch . . .

Interlude

Juvenile Detention Center

 **Wednesday, July 24**

Son, brother, friend. Archer, drummer.

Murderer.

Faces.

Why won't they go away? Daisy's, Hannah's, Lindsay's.

Ross's.

Zorro's.

Gray banged his fist against the steel door, then rubbed his hand over its wire-reinforced glass window, trying to erase the faces.

Lindsay, he thought.

Hannah.

Daisy.

Silently, but deafeningly inside his head, Gray screamed, *"I'm not sorry! Zorro deserved to die. If he hadn't done what he did to me, I'd never have shot anyone. It's Zorro's fault that other people got in the way."*

Epilogue

Superior Court

Thursday, November 7
Sentencing

Gray Wilton sat at the defense table, rigid, as if frozen in time. His face showed nothing, least of all the thoughts that were making staccato whirlpools in his mind.

Yeah, that jury was okay; they knew the score, knew no one else killed those kids, paid them back—well, not Hannah, maybe not really Ross—paid the others back like I had to.

Gray clasped his hands together, then dug what was left of his nails into his palms, pushing his fingers down one by one, silently counting, *One . . . two . . . three . . . four . . .*

Mr. Falco put his hand over Gray's and squeezed; Gray pulled away.

Wish I'd gotten me, too.

Sounded good at first, "tried as an adult." Cool. Yeah, but they kept saying "only fifteen, fourteen then" stuff like that; that's not cool. Can't fry me anyway, can't fry a kid; so where's the adult part, what good is it?

Mr. Falco leaned across Gray, saying something to his assistant. "Nervous," Gray thought he heard, and something about "remorse," or maybe it was "no remorse." Gray wasn't sure.

Well, it's Zorro's fault, really, and Johnson's. Damn Johnson, escaping. Yeah, okay, Dad's fault, too; maybe I should've gone for him first. But especially Zorro's fault. If it hadn't been for him and Johnson, no one would've gotten hurt.

Four counts of murder and one count of assault with intent to murder. That's Lindsay's, count number five. All hers. Hey, even though she can't walk, she lived. Not much of a life for her, everyone says, but hell, looks like Pete still wants to marry her someday, so she's gotten what I bet she most wanted. Yeah, it's too bad she can't walk, but Zorro's to blame for that, him and Johnson.

If they let me off, I'd sure like to get Johnson, too.

Would I do it?

Yeah, maybe.

"Gray," Mr. Falco whispered, "stand up, son, here's the judge."

Gray pushed himself to his feet, surprised that his knees felt weak, as if they weren't going to hold him. He swallowed against sudden nausea; he licked his dry lips.

Okay, now here it comes. Look at all the times Falco said, "Only fifteen; fourteen when it happened." And Falco said I was teased. Brutalized, he said. Misunderstood.

Yeah. So I showed them.

Bet I'll just get a couple of years in some jail, with maybe, I don't know, Ms. Throckmorton types, lots of TV. Guys where I'm going prob'ly saw me on TV back when they nabbed me, maybe back when the trial started, too; there were cameras outside when they walked me in. Wonder if Jemmy saw; his mom always made him watch the news. Big celebrity, right? Even though they sure didn't build a memorial to me at GHS. Wonder if they would've if I'd offed myself. They'd have been sorry then, I bet, maybe finally gotten it, understood. "Poor kid," they'd have said.

I bet they don't have hexagon windows in a real jail; won't have to go through that again—Lindsay's face, Hannah's, Daisy's, Ross's, Zorro's, staring, staring all the time . . . Best thing was offing him, offing Zorro.

Hurry up, Judge! Why's he leaning over like that? Who's he whispering to?

Oh. Falco.

Yeah, that's what he'll give me, betcha. A couple of years, couple of years for "only a troubled kid, only fifteen, only fourteen when he did it." So what that this was an adult trial! Different rules, that's all. The other guy, the lawyer against me, wasn't as good as Falco. All that stuff about me being evil, about "grieving parents, promising young lives cut down," blah, blah, blah. Jeez, Zorro was the evil one, you know? Falco as good as said that anyway, and then he went through all the troubled kid stuff. "Disturbed," he said. "Seriously disturbed. Depressed. Unnoticed. Neglected. Misunderstood." Yeah. Damn right, Mr. Judge! Misunderstood and neglected by everyone, even Dad, Falco said. And bullied, especially by Zorro. No more, though. Zorro won't be bullying anyone now, not anymore, not ever. Lotsa kids got old Misunderstood Disturbed Kid me to thank for that, right?

Mr. Falco returned to the defense table and put his arm across Gray's shoulders as the judge leaned back, rustling papers. "It's okay to sit again now, son. Look. Your mom's smiling at you."

Gray glanced across the courtroom and for a moment his eyes locked on to his mother's. Her smile was faint and sad. He turned away quickly, but not so quickly that he didn't notice his father sitting next to her. His mother had been at the trial every day, but Gray still hadn't seen his father except that one time shortly after the arraignment. His father's face was immobile, and he was looking at the judge, not at Gray. Peter had come to the trial a few times, and today Lindsay was there, too, sitting next to Peter in her wheelchair, holding Peter's hand. With his other hand, Peter gave Gray what looked like a thumbs-up sign.

What the hell's that for? Encouragement?

Maybe Pete's heard, heard they're gonna send me to jail for only a couple years, could just about take that, no longer, though. Then they'll let me out, and then I can get me a gun and finish the job. On Johnson, maybe. Maybe on me. Or maybe, maybe just go home. Yeah, maybe. Start again?

Maybe not. Sure didn't work last time. Shit. I don't know anymore.

Guess I never did.

See, the thing is, I had to. There wasn't any other way. No other way out, you know? They must've understood that, the jury. Sure, they said I did it, but that's a no-brainer. And they said I wasn't crazy, that I knew it was wrong. But they have to know it was just a mistake about Lindsay, an accident, you know, Hannah, too, and I guess Ross; I guess he was really okay. Shit. And okay, maybe I shouldn't've just shot without aiming for a minute at the end; got carried away I guess. Still, everyone would've been okay if it hadn't been for Zorro. Yeah, try him, ha, ha . . .

Mr. Falco patted Gray's arm and whispered, "Gray, it's time. Stand up again."

Something clutched at Gray's throat as the judge started speaking. He felt dizzy and even more nauseous, like maybe he was going to be sick right in the middle of the defense table, all over Mr. Falco's yellow pads. He swallowed hard again, made his face stay still, and tried to concentrate on what the judge was saying.

But he was too dizzy and the words were too hard. He looked away across the courtroom where he saw Ross's nice mom looking at him as if she didn't understand, and Lindsay's parents from next door, and what he guessed were Hannah's and Daisy's, and Zorro's mother and stepfather—they were all sitting together, many of them holding hands, looking sad, scared, angry. Ross's mom's eyes caught his and Gray looked away quickly. The judge seemed to be shuffling papers, talking to someone, and Gray's heart speeded up and the coppery fear-taste filled his mouth again. He turned toward his own parents, whose heads were close together, whispering, excluding him. Why couldn't they look at him? He glanced around at all the people, waiting, waiting tensely, eagerly, to hear what the judge was going to do to him, and he wanted to run, run out of the courtroom, run far away, and he started to move, but Mr. Falco gripped his arm, and Gray turned his head, desperately this time, toward his parents, his brother . . .

Dad . . . ugly stare . . . Jesus, tears, Mom's crying, why's she crying? Is he going to fry me after all? Wait, they can't do that to kids! . . . Is that what he just said? . . . No, he's going "only fifteen" again, "deeply disturbed," all that stuff . . . Come on, get to it, say it, damn him, damnit, damnit! Come on, do it! Look, I . . . I had to,

*anyone would've . . . What'd he just say? Maximum
something, maximum! . . . Christ, oh, Christ, come on,
time to go home . . . Mom, shit, stop crying! Dad, Pete,
Mom . . . Look, I'm sorry, okay? I'm okay, I'll be okay
now that Zorro's gone, you'll see, you'll all see . . .
Please . . . please, God! Please, really, I'll be good, I will,
Zorro's gone. Okay? Let's go, let's go home now . . .*

"Gray, no. Son, stay still, stay still. Shh, listen!"

". . . Life, without parole . . ."

*Oh, shit, oh, God! No, look, I couldn't . . . couldn't
fight them, couldn't . . . I said I'm sorry! Didn't I say it?
God, please . . .*

Please . . .